COUNTRY
LEGACY

SHIPMENT 1

Courted by the Cowboy by Sasha Summers
A Valentine for the Cowboy by Rebecca Winters
The Maverick's Bridal Bargain by Christy Jeffries
A Baby for the Deputy by Cathy McDavid
Safe in the Lawman's Arms by Patricia Johns
The Rancher and the Baby by Marie Ferrarella

SHIPMENT 2

Cowboy Doctor by Rebecca Winters
Rodeo Rancher by Mary Sullivan
The Cowboy Takes a Wife by Trish Milburn
A Baby for the Sheriff by Mary Leo
The Kentucky Cowboy's Baby by Heidi Hormel
Her Cowboy Lawman by Pamela Britton

SHIPMENT 3

A Texas Soldier's Family by Cathy Gillen Thacker
A Baby on His Doorstep by Roz Denny Fox
The Rancher's Surprise Baby by Trish Milburn
A Cowboy to Call Daddy by Sasha Summers
Made for the Rancher by Rebecca Winters
The Rancher's Baby Proposal by Barbara White Daille
The Cowboy and the Baby by Marie Ferrarella

SHIPMENT 4

Her Stubborn Cowboy by Patricia Johns
Texas Lullaby by Tina Leonard
The Texan's Little Secret by Barbara White Daille
The Texan's Surprise Son by Cathy McDavid
It Happened One Wedding Night by Karen Rose Smith
The Cowboy's Convenient Bride by Donna Alward

SHIPMENT 5

The Baby and the Cowboy SEAL by Laura Marie Altom
The Bull Rider's Cowgirl by April Arrington
Having the Cowboy's Baby by Judy Duarte
The Reluctant Texas Rancher by Cathy Gillen Thacker
A Baby on the Ranch by Marie Ferrarella
When the Cowboy Said "I Do" by Crystal Green

SHIPMENT 6

Aidan: Loyal Cowboy by Cathy McDavid
The Hard-to-Get Cowboy by Crystal Green
A Maverick to (Re)Marry by Christine Rimmer
The Maverick's Baby-in-Waiting by Melissa Senate
Unmasking the Maverick by Teresa Southwick
The Maverick's Christmas to Remember by Christy Jeffries

SHIPMENT 7

The Maverick Fakes a Bride! by Christine Rimmer
The Maverick's Bride-to-Order by Stella Bagwell
The Maverick's Return by Marie Ferrarella
The Maverick's Snowbound Christmas by Karen Rose Smith
The Maverick & the Manhattanite by Leanne Banks
A Maverick under the Mistletoe by Brenda Harlen
The Maverick's Christmas Baby by Victoria Pade

SHIPMENT 8

A Maverick and a Half by Marie Ferrarella
The More Mavericks, the Merrier! by Brenda Harlen
From Maverick to Daddy by Teresa Southwick
A Very Maverick Christmas by Rachel Lee
The Texan's Christmas by Tanya Michaels
The Cowboy SEAL's Christmas Baby by Laura Marie Altom

COUNTRY
LEGACY

THE MAVERICK'S
SNOWBOUND
CHRISTMAS

USA TODAY BESTSELLING AUTHOR

Karen Rose Smith

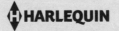

Special thanks and acknowledgment are given to
Karen Rose Smith for her contribution to the
Montana Mavericks: The Great Family Roundup continuity.

PLEASE RECYCLE · THIS PRODUCT IS RECYCLABLE

Recycling programs
for this product may
not exist in your area.

ISBN-13: 978-1-335-52354-9

The Maverick's Snowbound Christmas
First published in 2017. This edition published in 2022.
Copyright © 2017 by Harlequin Enterprises ULC

For questions and comments about the quality of this book,
please contact us at CustomerService@Harlequin.com.

Harlequin Enterprises ULC
22 Adelaide St. West, 41st Floor
Toronto, Ontario M5H 4E3, Canada
www.Harlequin.com

Printed in U.S.A.

USA TODAY bestselling author **Karen Rose Smith** has written over ninety novels. Her passion is caring for her four rescued cats, and her hobbies are gardening, cooking and photography. An only child, Karen delved into books at an early age. Even though she escaped into story worlds, she had many cousins around her on weekends. Families are a strong theme in her novels. Find out more about Karen at karenrosesmith.com.

To my veterinarians, Drs. Brian and Jessica, who treat my cats with expertise and caring.

Chapter 1

Eli Dalton ran his hand over his pregnant mare's side. He breathed in the scents of leather, straw, old wood and the dampness from snow that had begun to fall. Worry niggled in his gut. He'd been around horses all his life, and something just didn't seem right with Amber's labor. She'd been a wild mustang, and he'd gentled her himself. He couldn't let something go wrong. He couldn't lose her foal.

Leaving her for a few moments to get some perspective, he went to the barn door and peered out. Two or three inches of snow had already fallen. Any other time, somebody else would be around to give him an opinion. Of course, this weekend of all weekends, everyone was gone from the ranch. His parents had left for Missoula for an equipment auction, and Derek, the only sibling who was still living at home, had gone with them, as had his uncle and cousins. One of his sisters, Kristen, might have been some help, but she'd flown to LA with her husband to celebrate an early Thanksgiving with him. Eli's gaze ran over the miles of fencing on the Circle D. Ranching and caring for horses had been embedded deeply in his soul from before he could remember.

He heard a noise coming from Amber's stall. She was down. He rushed to her and ran his hand over her belly...looked into her eyes. She whinnied at him, and he knew there was only one thing to do. Call the veterinarian.

"Don't you know your biological clock is ticking?"

Hadley Strickland pushed her wavy dark brown hair away from her face and glanced around the kitchen at the dishes being prepared for the Strickland clan, wondering how to exit this conversation. Her sister Tessa, who lived in LA, had a vacation home on

Falls Mountain and was here for Thanksgiving, didn't hesitate to probe, question or bully. Ever since she'd found her "happily-ever-after," she was worse. Hadley was just glad her sister Claire wasn't in the kitchen right now to weigh in on this conversation as well.

Hadley cast her dark brown eyes on her grandmother Melba Strickland, who was matriarchal and grandmotherly all at the same time. But her grandmother was no help at all because she asked, "Have you dated in the past few months?"

There were so many ways to answer that question. Hadley put in long hours at the veterinary clinic where she worked in Bozeman. She often covered for other vets when it wasn't her turn in the rotation. She kept up on all the latest vetcrinary journals. On top of all that, she was qualifying for her pilot's license. However, the simplest answer could usually turn the subject of the conversation in another direction much faster. She didn't want anybody dwelling on her personal life.

She added cherry tomatoes to the salad she'd been fixing and said offhandedly, "I'm too busy to date."

As a small animal vet, she was thinking of expanding horizons by owning her own practice someday. But for now, if she became a pilot, she might be able to help animals at a greater distance or in the wild. She knew someday her life would come together. But she also knew it might never include romance again. Her family didn't know her secret, a secret that was embarrassing and showed how foolish a woman could be when she was wildly attracted to a man.

She could see Tessa was gearing up for another question when the cell phone attached to Hadley's belt buzzed. She kept it there from habit because she was never without it. Gratefully, she plucked it out of its case, gave a sheepish smile to her grandmother and sister and checked the screen.

"It's Brooks Smith," she murmured. He was the town's main veterinarian. She always stopped in when she was in Rust Creek Falls to check out his practice and talk to him about the latest advances in animal care. She even helped him now and then. Maybe he wanted to set up a time they could get together while she was in town. He and his wife, Jazzy, ran a horse rescue ranch, and Hadley was always fascinated by the work they did there.

She held up her finger to her sister and

grandmother, indicating she was going to take the call. "Hi, Brooks," she said.

"Hey, Hadley. How are you?"

"I'm good. What's up?"

"I need a favor."

"What can I do?"

"I'm tied up on a ranch near Kalispell. Dr. Wellington, a vet working with me, quit unexpectedly, and my backup vet, my dad, just had knee replacement surgery."

Hadley knew Brooks and his dad coordinated their practices even though they were in separate locations. Brooks's dad had been gearing back, hoping to retire soon.

"What's the favor?" Maybe he wanted her to go in and check on animals at his practice.

"There's a mare in labor at the Circle D, and Eli thinks she's in trouble. No obvious signs, but he knows horses. She's down in her stall, and he's worried."

Her grandfather, Old Gene as he was called, came into the kitchen and was studying the women with a probing eye. He spotted Hadley on the phone.

"So you want me to drive to the Dalton ranch and see if he needs help?"

"That sums it up. I know it's snowing and

you're spending time with your family, but Eli wouldn't put out a call without good reason."

"I have all-wheel drive. I'll be fine. Does he know you're calling me?"

"He doesn't know I'm specifically calling *you*. I told him I'd try to get somebody out there. I'll call him back and let him know. Thanks for doing this, Hadley. I owe you."

"You owe me nothing. You know, Brooks, I mostly handle small animals. Horses aren't my specialty."

"You're a vet, Hadley. That counts right now. I'll tell Eli you're coming, and I'll text you his number in case you need it."

Drew and Benjamin, two of Hadley's cousins who were here for Thanksgiving, suddenly made an appearance in the kitchen doorway. Hosting family for the holidays, her grandparents had a full house. Drew and Benjamin were over six feet tall, and with their sudden male presence, the kitchen seemed very small.

"Are you really going out in this?" Old Gene asked.

Drew studied her with a worried expression. "This is supposed to be a monster storm. We could get a lot of snow in a short amount of time."

"Then I'd better get going," she said. "There's a mare who needs me."

And before anyone else could protest or stop her, she left the kitchen to dress in warmer clothes and boots.

Hadley veered down the lane to the Circle D, her vehicle's tires churning up snow as she drove. She'd almost been relieved to leave her grandmother's boardinghouse, and that was unusual. She enjoyed being with family. But on this visit there seemed to be pressure from her sisters, her grandparents and even her cousins to talk about her love life. She had *no* love life—with very good reason. No one knew why, and she wasn't about to reveal it. Her parents were supposed to arrive for Thanksgiving next week, and that would mean even more pressure.

Pressure for what? Finding Mr. Right when Mr. Right didn't exist? Pressure to be some woman she wasn't? Pressure to get hurt again?

She took the fork in the lane that led to the house and barn. She assumed that if the mare was having problems, that's where Eli Dalton would be. She thought about this rancher who was supposed to be one of the eligible bachelors in town. Their paths had crossed now and then, most recently at his sister Kayla's wedding. But there were so many cowboys and ranchers in Rust Creek Falls that Hadley didn't pay much attention to him. After all, she wasn't looking.

As she climbed down from her vehicle and slammed the door, complete silence surrounded her. There wasn't a creature stirring. Snow fell more heavily now, and she supposed they'd all taken cover as best they could. Montana was beautiful, but the winters could be harsh. Most humans and creatures living here knew how to survive and thrive. She was still trying to figure out the thrive part.

Opening the back door of her SUV, she grabbed her bag, closed the door and trudged to the barn. After she opened the door, her eyes adjusted to the dimmer light. As they did, she took in the scents—horses, hay, aged wood. She took a few more steps forward, and then she saw him. Eli Dalton was leaning low over his horse. She assumed it was his horse. The way he was caressing her, she saw so much caring just in the stroke of his hand. He was murmuring to her, encouraging her, and something in his tone made Hadley's throat tighten. That was silly. She'd seen a man's kindness to a horse before.

Eli's hair was dark brown, thick, and fell over his brow as he leaned forward. He knelt by the horse's back, his own back long and lean as he bent down to the horse's belly and put his ear to it. His shoulders were so broad. Although he was kneeling, she could tell his legs were long. He was wearing the requisite worn cowboy boots that looked like his favorite pair. His navy insulated vest fell open over his green-and-navy flannel shirt. He was so focused on the horse, he was totally unaware that she'd come in.

She made sure her boots made a scuffling noise as she approached him.

He looked up as if startled from his concentration.

"I'm Hadley Strickland," she said in explanation. "Brooks Smith called me to help you."

He looked torn, as if he wanted to stand and approach her, yet he didn't want to leave the horse. To help him with that dilemma, she went to him.

He held out his hand to her.

"I'm Eli Dalton. We met at Kayla's wedding briefly. In the receiving line."

As Hadley shook his hand and gazed into his eyes, her world seemed to spin a little faster. His grip was firm and warm and urged her breaths to come faster. Recognizing the red flags of attraction, she pulled her hand out of his clasp. "There was a lot of chatter and bedlam at the wedding," she murmured for something to say. "That's a wedding for you."

He gave her an odd look, and she changed the subject. "So what seems to be the problem?" She looked over the horse again from her golden-brown coat to the white blaze, from her forelock to her nose.

"I'm not sure. Amber is a wild mustang I adopted. I gentled her. I've been with her every day. I've been around pregnant horses since I was three, and I know what pregnancy and labor is supposed to look like."

"What are the signs that make you think something's wrong?"

"This is a maiden mare from what I can tell, so I know she can foal a bit early or late. She's not particularly high-strung, so I don't think she's resisting the normal process of delivery. Her udder has been swollen for the last five weeks. I've been cleaning her with warm cloths."

"And she let you?"

"She trusts me."

Hadley took that in. As she knelt beside Eli, she saw the thickened nipple. They naturally developed a thick waxy material. When the nipple got waxed, that was an indicator that the foal would be born within the next day or so. Even though Hadley didn't often handle large animals, she knew each mare was unique. All the owner could do would be to evaluate all the signs for an impending foaling.

"Will she let me examine her?" Hadley asked.

"If I stay here and talk to her, she will."

"All right, let me get my gloves on and we'll do it."

Hadley tried to forget that Eli was there as she checked signs of the rump and tail-head muscles softening. "Any changes in behavior?"

"She's been more affectionate latcly and separated herself from the other horses."

"What about appetite?"

"She hasn't eaten today."

"I see you laid down straw."

"I'll switch it to shavings a few days after birth. Usually this is a natural process, but something's bothering me about it."

"Nothing specific?"

"No, but I didn't want to get in trouble with the snowstorm. It was better to have someone here to help than me not having the expertise to handle anything unusual that comes along."

Aha, Hadley thought. Eli was a planner. Rumor had it that he was steady and responsible. His attitude today proved it.

Hadley continued her examination, then stripped off her gloves and put her stethoscope back in her bag. "All we can do is wait. This could be a couple of hours, maybe more."

They both heard the howl of the wind against the side of the barn. "Maybe you should leave. Go back to the boardinghouse while you can still get out."

"Brooks is a friend, Mr. Dalton. He asked me to help so I'm here to help. I'm staying."

Eli had to be a good six foot four. She was only five foot four. He studied her with probing green eyes from her green jacket to her cowl-necked pullover sweater to her skinny blue jeans and boots. "All right," he said, "But call me Eli."

"And I'm Hadley."

He nodded. "It's good to have backup here, Hadley. Thanks for coming out. Have you eaten lunch?"

"No. I didn't think to grab anything to bring along."

"I'll go up to the house and get us something." He nodded to the horse. "We have to keep up our strength so we can help her."

"Amber, did you say?" she asked.

"Her coat's that color," he explained. "And her eyes."

A man who noticed the color of a horse's eyes. Eli Dalton was intriguing her more and more.

As Eli trudged through four inches of snow to the farmhouse, he knew he shouldn't feel hot. It was just the stress of worrying about Amber. It wasn't his blood running faster every time he looked at Hadley Strickland.

Although he'd more than noticed her when they'd crossed paths in the past, he'd never gone out of his way to chat her up. There was good reason for that. He knew her type all too well. She was educated and career-minded just as Elaine had been. His thoughts wanted to take him back twelve years, but he resisted as he always did. He had no intention of ever getting involved with a woman like that again. Since then, "serious" hadn't been on his mind.

He knocked the snow from his boots before he went into the house. Once inside, it didn't take him long. His mom always had the refrigerator stocked. After all, hungry ranch hands needed fuel. He scooped together sandwiches with thick bread and lots of meat and cheese, then slipped them into ziplock bags and put those into a grocery bag. He grabbed packets of mayonnaise and mustard from the refrigerator shelf. His mom kept plenty in there to put in lunch boxes for when they were out for the day fixing fence or other repairs. Next, he brewed coffee. When it was ready, he poured it into a large thermos, grabbed a tin of cookies, a few foam cups and paper dishes, then pushed everything into another grocery bag. Picking up both bags and the thermos, he headed out again.

In the barn once more, Eli spotted Hadley standing at Amber's stall. The mare was back on her feet.

"She's not ready," Hadley said. "I think she's trying to help herself."

"You mean let gravity help her," Eli amended.

Hadley looked at him then, her gaze locking to his.

He felt a jolt of elemental attraction that he attempted to dismiss.

"I told you I don't have a lot of experience with horses," she reminded him.

With difficulty, he transferred his focus to Amber again rather than Hadley and gave her an out if she wanted it. "I hate to tie you up here if it's not necessary."

"But you're still worried."

Apparently she could read him. He didn't like that. Over the past dozen years, he'd dated...but never seriously. He tried *not* to let women read him. Still, he answered her truthfully. "I am worried. Not only about Amber. The snow's getting deeper, and you might not be able to get out if you don't go now."

She laid her hand on his forearm. "I think taking care of a horse in labor is more important than my getting back to town."

The sincerity in her voice rocked him almost as much as the feel of her hand on his arm.

They stood awkwardly for a few moments because they both knew what Hadley staying would entail. They'd be cooped up here together, almost perfect strangers who knew nothing about each other. She pulled her hand away from him.

They might be strangers, but he was becoming more curious about her.

"Come on," he said. "Let's go into the tack room and have some lunch. Dad had that area of the barn renovated so he could use it as an office as well as a tack room. He made sure it was safe for a gas-fed infrared heater. It's not toasty, but it's warmer than the barn."

Hadley followed him to the tack room.

"Living in Montana, I'm sure you've been snowed in before." They might as well get to know something about each other.

"I have," she agreed with a nod. "If I'm at the clinic, I keep the animals company. I've always been able to entertain myself with a good book, and I carry one wherever I go."

"Do you have one with you now?" he asked as he pulled a wood captain's chair next to the desk chair.

"I have one in the SUV."

Hadley was glancing around, and Eli tried to see the tack room area through her eyes. It was orderly with saddles on sawhorses and harnesses and bridles hanging on pegs on the wall. The concrete floor, absent of straw or any debris, made the space safe for the heater. The heater kept the room between fifty-five and sixty degrees when it was running. He kept his jacket hanging on a peg behind the door. If it came to it, Hadley could use his coat as well as her own. Eli's gaze swept from the computer and flat-screen monitor on the scarred wood desk back to her.

She caught him watching her. "What?"

"I just wondered if you were cold." He reached for the bag of sandwiches to give his hands something to do. For some reason, he was so tempted to push back the waves of her hair from her cheek. That was a crazy idea.

"I'm cold-weather friendly," she told him with a smile. "Even though I spend most of my hours in the clinic with small animals, I do like to hike and cross-country ski."

He arched his brows. "Good to know."

A few minutes later he'd laid out everything he brought into the tack room and poured the coffee into the insulated cups. She looked at all of it a bit wide-eyed.

"What's wrong?" he asked.

Her cheeks reddened. "This is really thoughtful."

He chuckled. "Making a few sandwiches and brewing coffee?"

"You brought chips and cookies, too."

There was something in her voice that made him study her. "Why do you think that's thoughtful? I need to eat as well as you."

"Never mind," she said, her cheeks growing a little redder.

He handed her a sandwich. "We could be here a while. We need stuff to talk about. Feel free to spill anything you want."

Now she laughed. "It's no deep, dark secret."

Although those were the words that came from her very pretty lips, a shadow passed over her eyes. That shadow convinced Eli that maybe Hadley Strickland *did* have secrets. He waited.

"I've just come to expect men to think about themselves first."

To lighten the mood, he grinned at her. "I did. I was hungry."

She gave him a steady look. "Let's just say I think your momma taught you well."

That gave him pause. "She did," he agreed. "Though with my brother Derek, I'm not sure he had his ears open."

Hadley laughed. "He *does* have a reputation."

"You've heard about it from Melba and Old Gene? Or maybe your sisters?"

"My sisters mostly. Not that we talk about men every time we get together." There was amusement in her voice, and he wondered what they *did* talk about. Family? Their goals and dreams?

After taking a few bites of his sandwich and having a swallow of coffee, he asked, "How long are you staying in Rust Creek Falls?"

"I plan to stay until after Thanksgiving. My mom and dad will be joining the rest of the clan here." When she said it, she wrinkled her nose slightly. When she did, he noticed freckles on her cheeks. She had such a beautiful natural look.

He cleared his throat and asked, "You're not glad your mom and dad are coming?"

She looked thoughtful for a moment then shrugged. "Oh, I love spending time with Mom and Dad and the rest of my family. It's just that sometimes they gang up on me because my life isn't as settled as theirs. As long as I can keep the conversation on everybody else, we're good."

In the silence that followed, Hadley's cell phone beeped. She'd opened her coat, and now she pulled the phone from a holder on her belt. Eli couldn't help but glimpse under her coat—at her softly rounded breasts, her slim waist. She wasn't tall either. Just how well did she handle the animals she treated?

When she seemed to hesitate about answering the call or text message, he encouraged her to do it. "You'd better use your phone while you can. Service is spotty out here on the best days, and on days like this, it can cut out anytime."

She checked her phone and smiled. "It's my grandmother. She wants to know if I got here safely." Her thumbs worked the small keyboard, and then she returned to eating her sandwich.

"What did you tell Melba?"

"That I'm midwifing and don't know when I'll be back."

"And you added, *Don't worry about me*," he guessed.

"You obviously understand the protective family."

"I'm protective myself at times." After all, he was the oldest. He'd learned responsibility at a young age. He'd not only learned it but accepted it. Taking care of those around him came naturally to him.

Suddenly Hadley put her sandwich down and looked over her shoulder.

"What is it?"

She put her finger to her lips to shush him, and seemed to listen intently. Then she got to her feet and was careful to step softly toward the shelves to the rear of the tack room.

"A field mouse could have made its way in here," he began.

But Hadley paid no attention. Instead she bent over to the lowest shelf, moved a box of grooming equipment and scooped up something. When she turned around, in her arms she held a kitten.

At that moment, Eli knew he was in big trouble. Hadley Strickland standing there with a kitten in the crook of her arm was a sight that made his blood run fast and his heart increase its rhythm. Just what he didn't need—an attraction to a well-educated woman who probably considered ranch life foreign to her. He had to get his libido under control and do it *fast*.

Chapter 2

Hadley walked toward Eli, and for a few seconds he thought about backing up. But he couldn't. He was mesmerized by her and the kitten in her arms.

As she stood in front of him, she handed him the kitten. "Can you hold her? I think the mom is back there, too."

What choice did he have? Along with catching Hadley's vanilla scent that was so different from the perfumes women usually wore, besides being close enough to think about touching her hair that looked even softer than he originally thought it might be, besides staring at her lips for a nanosecond and imagining—

Coming back to reality with a jolt, he took the kitten and nestled it on his forearm. It was adorable with colors split on its face. One side was tan, the other dark brown into black. All shades from gold to brown melded in its coat.

Hadley's gaze met his, and they seemed locked in the moment. Then her focus went to the kitten. She brushed her thumb under its eye.

"She's too little to be separated from her mom, so if we make friends with one, we have to make friends with both." With that she swiftly turned and went back to the shelves. In another minute, she had another cat in her arms, a lighter tortoiseshell, one that hardly looked old enough to have a litter of kittens.

"Do you think they're hungry?" Eli asked. "There's cat food in the cupboard." He motioned to the storage units near the shelves.

"Stray cats are usually always hungry," Hadley agreed. "The little one should be old enough to eat a bit of cat food mixed with water. You haven't seen them around before?"

"Barn cats come and go. My guess is they hide whenever humans come in. If I see them, I feed them." He gave a shrug. "But I haven't seen these two before."

"They probably took shelter in here from the cold and the snow. They need to be tested, and the little one looks as if she might need eyedrops."

"We can do that," he said. "They're not going to get out of the barn now, that's for sure."

Hadley settled the momma cat on the chair. Instead of scampering away like Eli might have expected she would do, she sat there and looked up at Hadley, as if grateful for the company and the attention.

"What about the kitten?" he asked. "Should I just put her down?"

"Do you have a box and maybe an old blanket? We can make her a better bed. After she eats, she might sleep there, depending on the mom."

"You said they need to be tested. What are you testing for?"

"Feline leukemia and FIV."

"And if they have it?"

"We'll talk after they're tested. No use jumping the gun."

Eli handed Hadley the kitten, understanding that she dealt with this every day—clients bringing pets for her care, clients losing pets, clients hoping Hadley could make everything better. He found the food, then emptied a box that held old tack that needed repair. In no time, he'd created a bed with a fleece saddle pad.

Eli searched for something they could use for dishes. He borrowed the lid to a jar that held organic cookie treats for the horses. It was big enough that both mom and kitten could eat from it.

Handing it to Hadley along with a bottle of water from a case on the floor, he said, "This is the best I could do."

"This will work great. Are you sure you've never done this before?"

"There's a first time for everything."

When their eyes met, Eli thought he caught a flash of attraction in Hadley's brown gaze. He knew *he* was feeling it. Maybe it was just the idea of being cooped up during a snowstorm that made their awareness of each other so intense.

"I'll check on Amber," he said gruffly and exited the tack room to do just that.

Hadley told herself to focus on what she was doing while Eli checked on his horse. Why did her gaze want to follow him? Eli drew her eyes to him like he was a magnet and she was the weakest piece of metal. It wasn't just his broad shoulders, though they *were* broad. It wasn't his slim hips and his flat stomach under his vest, though she could imagine a six-pack under his flannel shirt. It wasn't his long legs encased in jeans that fit oh, so well. How often had she seen cowboys in jeans? Eli's jeans looked as if they were comfortable, worn white in some places. She *had* to stop sneaking peeks at him.

Focusing on the cat food and the water, she mixed it together in the lid. As soon as she lowered it to the floor, momma cat was there instantly and so was baby. Only baby seemed to be having a hard time of it. Not used to eating food from a dish? That was easily fixed.

Hadley dipped her finger into the mixture and held it to the kitten's nose. The kitten's little pink tongue snuck out and lapped at her finger. The hairs on the nape of her neck prickled, and she felt Eli's presence as soon as he was near. It wasn't his shadow. It wasn't the soapy leather scent that seemed to surround him. It was just…him. He was back and watching her.

Hadley knew about the cowboy kind. She'd dated a few. They were hardworking, but often narrow-minded, never looking at the world around them, only at the world they knew.

Eli hunkered down next to her and lifted the cat food can. "It looks like she needs a little more." He forked more food into the lid, his arm bumping hers.

Hadley poured more water from the bottle and almost spilled it. Being this close to Eli made her feel a bit shaky. How crazy was that?

"Do you really think they'll sleep in the box?" he asked.

As she turned to face him, her body was close to his. She took in the details of his face, the lines around his eyes, the slight furrow in his brow. There was a light scar on the left side of his cheek, and her fingers suddenly itched to touch it.

No, no, no, she told herself, turning away from him. She murmured, "They might. If Momma thinks it's cuddly, warm and safe."

Giving her attention once more to the momma cat and baby, she saw the kitten was eating from the dish now, having gotten the idea from tasting the food on Hadley's finger.

Feeling suddenly nervous around Eli, she needed something to say. "They'll probably sleep after they eat. If you put the box right near those shelves where they were, they'll probably settle there. They're creatures of habit just as we are."

She used a bit of the water to wash her fingers, and then wiped them on a napkin. She went to her bag that she'd dropped on the desk and took out a vial of antibacterial gel that needed no water and rubbed it on her hands. Then she hurriedly left the tack room to check on Eli's mustang.

Immediately, Hadley saw that Amber didn't seem to be in any distress. Maybe Eli had been all wrong about a problem with labor. Maybe she should leave while she could.

On the other hand, she sighed at the thought of being around a whole boardinghouse full of Stricklands. Maybe the truth was that it was getting harder to keep her secret from her family. In some ways, she wanted to talk to her sisters about it. Yet in others, she still felt ashamed and foolish about a romance that had been so wrong. No one really needed to know what she'd done. Not ever. But keeping her past romantic mistake to herself sometimes made her feel as if there was a wall between her and her family.

As she walked back to the tack room, she glimpsed Eli setting the box near the shelves. Joining him, she watched the momma cat walk toward the box and the baby follow. Momma circled a few times, hopped in and kneaded the saddle pad. Baby hopped in with her. Soon she was suckling her mom.

With a smile that made Hadley feel tingly all over, Eli studied the cats with her. Then he asked about Amber. Though she told him the mare was fine, he obviously needed to see for himself.

In the barn once more, he ran practiced hands over Amber's flanks. "She's restless, but not pushing. I don't know what happened earlier. She's even eaten a little."

"We'll keep watching her," Hadley assured him.

The gusts of wind outside suddenly became more forceful. The side door of the barn blew open, and more than one horse whinnied.

"I'll get it," Hadley said, rushing toward the door.

"Put the bar across," Eli called to her. "Or do you want me to do it?"

"I can do it," she called back. She might be short and slender, but she was strong. She worked out with weights when she could. She had to stay strong to lift animals, even though she was a small animal vet. Sometimes she had to handle German shepherds that could weigh ninety or a hundred pounds.

The vehemence of the wind pushed against

the door, and she pushed back, closing it with a bang. She hefted up the plank of wood beside the doorjamb and swung it into place. She glanced toward the other end of the barn, where, luckily, the large airplane hangar-style door was securely latched. When the wind blew, the plank rumbled a little, but it wasn't going anywhere. She couldn't see out of the high windows up above. Falling snow completely blocked them.

Eli came out from the stall. "That was impressive. Do you handle elephants in your small pet practice?"

She laughed. "No, but I try not to let the big dogs run away with me. I had to lift a pregnant Newfoundland once. Ever since then, I've kept up my strength. It comes in handy at times like these."

He beckoned to the tack room. "Come on, let's finish our lunch. Maybe nibbling on those cookies will help us forget about the wind howling outside. Are you nervous being in here?"

Following him to the warmest spot in the barn, she sat in the captain's chair and watched as he poured coffee into the top of the thermos and handed that cup to her. He used a foam cup for himself.

"Nervous?" she asked. "You mean about the storm?"

"About the storm, about being cooped up in here with a relative stranger, about not knowing when you'll get out."

She motioned to the heater. "We have heat." She gestured to the cookie tin. "We have food." She pointed to the water. "We even have bottled water. That's more than a lot of people have on a daily basis. I think we'll survive. No, I'm not nervous." Though if she was really honest with herself, being this close to Eli in a confined space caused the jitters to plague her.

"How long did it take you to gentle Amber?" Conversation seemed the best way to calm them. She had to admit she wanted to know Eli better.

"It depends on what you mean by *gentling*," he explained. "It took about a week until she would come to the fence when I called. I just sat there and spoke to her in a low voice, not expecting anything from her. The next part of the gentling was treats. A hungry horse will want to get to know you faster. I ordered those organic cookies that are supposed to be good for horses. She definitely needed her share of vitamins. She took to them. I'd hold out one of those and she'd come right up. She was still skittish, but after another week or so of that, she let me touch her. First her neck, then her flank, then her nose. I would just go outside and sit with her and whittle."

"Whittle?"

He shrugged. "It's just a hobby of mine."

"So you took time out of your daily schedule to spend with Amber?"

"I did. How else was I going to get to know her, or let her get to know me?"

Hadley pulled one of the cookies from the tin to give herself something to do and something else to think about other than the sound of Eli's voice and the idea of him running a hand down Amber's flank. The cookie was chocolate chip, and she took a bite and savored it. "Great cookies."

"My mom knows how to bake."

"Melba does, too," Hadley said. "And she teaches me favorite recipes whenever I'm around her."

"Do you cook much for yourself?" Eli asked.

Hadley shook her head. "I'm rarely at my place. Mostly I pick up takeout. Sometimes on weekends I'll make a stew or soup, sticky buns or a loaf of bread. It isn't that I don't know how, it's just that I don't have time. I'm taking lessons for my pilot's license now. I have even less leisure time than before."

For some reason, Eli frowned. "A pilot's license. You sound like a woman who wants adventure."

Something about the edge to his voice told her he didn't think that was a good thing. "I don't know about wanting adventure. I just don't want my life to be static. Piloting a small plane could help me reach patients at a greater distance, even the wild horses if they need medical care. I haven't figured it all out yet. I just know I want to." Changing the subject away from her life, she said, "I understand you have cousins staying here now."

"I do, but I'm not in the mix too much. I built a cabin on my chunk of the ranch in late summer, so I have privacy when I want it. My brother Jonah designed it, and I worked on it myself."

"Did you decorate it, too?" She could imagine that it was a bachelor pad with a requisite big-screen TV, recliner, king-size bed and not much else.

But Eli answered her seriously. "My sister Kristen gave me some suggestions, but for the most part I went online and found the rest."

"You mean like stuff for the walls?"

"Why sound so surprised?" he asked with amusement twinkling in his eyes. "I like art and pottery. There's a wall hanging a friend of my mom's made. Or are you more surprised that I know how to use a computer? I'm a rancher, Hadley, but that doesn't mean I don't have other skills."

He seemed insulted when he said it, and she'd never meant for anything she'd said to be an insult. But she must have touched some kind of nerve because he definitely had withdrawn.

Taking a cookie from the tin, he stood. "If you could keep an eye on Amber, I'm going to check on the other horses. Just yell if you need me." Then he gave her a look. "Yell if Amber needs me. I have the feeling you're the type of woman who doesn't need anyone."

Leaving her sitting there with her mouth practically open, he left.

Eli had to admit he didn't know what had gotten into him. Maybe he'd just wanted to put some kind of wedge between himself and Hadley since they'd been thrown into this situation that had seemed to produce a potent attraction. Or maybe, truth be told, he'd never put his failed relationship with Elaine in the past. He thought he'd gotten over any insecurity he might have had about not going to college or seeking a higher education. At the time, he'd told himself it was an unnecessary expense and not essential to a good life. After all, he could read on his own, and he did. He knew about subjects from inorganic chemistry to horse husbandry, and he had traveled. He'd traveled with Elaine.

When she'd left, any wanderlust he might have had went with her. Hadley, with her education and expertise and adventurous spirit, had reopened past wounds without even knowing it. It wasn't her fault. She was who she was. The problem was—she was damned attractive. But she seemed to have an attitude that he was a cowboy, a rancher who couldn't see farther than the end of his nose. That's what had gotten under his skin. Granted, he was self-taught at computer skills, but he could master any program or app. He didn't care about just barbed wire and the best boots to wear on the ranch.

He was emptying a sack of feed into a bin when Hadley called to him. "Amber is down again."

Without hesitation, he rushed to the horse's

stall, wondering if this time the foal would be born or if something else was going on. He saw right away that Hadley had wrapped Amber's tail. Smart move, and he should have done it.

"Do you need the foaling kit?" he asked. He had one and kept it well stocked.

"No, I have my bag."

He could see the placental sac had broken. The pressure of Amber lying down had probably ruptured it.

"She's starting to push," Hadley said, kneeling on the straw beside Amber.

Eli knew this part of the labor. It should happen fairly quickly. If it didn't happen in an hour, then there *was* trouble.

Amber was making groaning sounds now, and Hadley was concentrating on her and what was happening. "I see it," Hadley said, and he knew she was talking about the white sac that covered the foal.

But Eli realized suddenly that this wasn't going to be a normal birth. The foal was in the breech position, hind feet first.

Crouched down beside Hadley, Eli asked her, "What's the best way to handle this?"

They both could see the hooves, and they were flexed upward toward the mare's tail.

"Are we going to lose it?" he asked, his chest feeling tight.

"We are *not* going to lose it," Hadley assured him. "Breech births are more difficult, but we can still make this as natural as possible without complications."

As Amber groaned, Eli's elbow brushed Hadley's. Their eyes locked for a moment, and he said huskily, "I'm glad you're here." He meant it, feeling something deeply comforting because of her presence. And it wasn't simply because she was a vet.

"I'm glad I'm here, too," she murmured. Then louder, she admitted, "I haven't done anything like this since an apprenticeship with a vet right after college. But I know what to do, Eli." This time Hadley pulled on gloves that reached to her elbows.

His thoughts seemed to be in an uproar until he pulled one free. "What are you going to do?"

"Just give her a little help if she needs it. Let's just see if nature takes its course. I don't want to step in if I don't have to."

He was experienced enough to know that letting nature take its course was the best route to take. Amber giving birth was a natural process. Yet he didn't want to lose either the foal or the mom.

The foal's hocks delivered, and Eli knew the foal's hips and tail would follow. Yet there seemed to be a problem, and Amber was straining hard.

Hadley murmured almost to herself, "The hips are the foal's widest part when delivery happens this way."

"Can you help? Can you get her baby unstuck?"

"I don't want to interfere too much, and I don't want to hurt either of them. I remember when Charlie did this..."

"Charlie?"

"The vet I worked with. He was seventy and had been delivering horses for almost forty years. I can picture exactly how he handled the birth. I'm going to grasp the foal's feet and just pull gently down toward Amber's hooves. That should rotate the foal's pelvis so it can pass through the birth canal more easily. Say a prayer."

As Hadley did what she said she was going to do, Eli did say a prayer. They both seemed to hold their breath as the foal slid out, making its appearance into the big wide world.

In the next few moments, Hadley removed an instrument from her bag and broke the sac surrounding the foal.

When Eli glanced at Hadley, he saw her eyes were misty. The birth of Amber's foal had touched her deeply. His throat constricted too because a miracle lay before them. What would have happened if Hadley hadn't been here?

"You saved them," he said, close enough to Hadley to kiss her.

She seemed to be eyeing his lips the same way he was eyeing hers. "You could have done the same thing," she whispered.

He got a whiff of that vanilla scent of hers that right now seemed as magical as an aphrodisiac. Shaking off the feeling and gathering his concentration, he conceded, "Maybe. But you knew what you were doing. I've only read about it."

Her eyes searched his face. "You were prepared for this?"

"I try to be prepared for everything. But I've never delivered a breech birth."

Awareness of the fact that he and Hadley seemed to be breathing in unison swept over him.

He was also aware of the way Hadley's bangs lay near her brows…aware of her high cheekbones…aware of the curve of her lips. With a supreme effort, he forced himself to focus on the situation at hand.

"They'll probably lie like this for ten to fifteen minutes," he said.

The horses needed to rest as the umbilical cord transferred a vital amount of blood from mare to foal. When that was complete, the cord would break on its own.

"I know," Hadley responded.

Her eyes were on his again, and she was close enough for their words to mix in the chilly air. Suddenly, she backed away. "Since we still have some waiting to do," she said, pulling off her gloves, "is there any more coffee?"

Now Hadley had refocused her gaze on the foal and his chocolate-brown coat. He had a white blaze like his mom.

"Do you see babies delivered often?" Eli asked.

"Mostly dogs and cats. It's been years since I was present at a foal's birth. I'm always in awe."

"Just wait until the little one starts to nurse. That's a sight to behold, too."

She nodded, her long dark hair slipping over her shoulder. "When a baby's born— dog, cat, horse—it's hard for humans not to want to step in, care for it, wipe down and cuddle it. But letting nature take its course and letting momma and baby bond is so important. Maybe that's why some women like to use midwives at home instead of going to the sterile noisy atmosphere of a hospital. Mother and baby can bond more easily."

"Could be." Eli had never really thought about that. But Hadley could be right. Hospitals, antiseptic walls, nurses and doctors could muddle up the whole process.

He would have stepped away then to go fetch the coffee for their wait, but Hadley took hold of his arm. Her touch through the flannel of his shirt caused a reaction inside him he hadn't felt for a very long time.

She said, "I'm glad you called Brooks, and I'm glad he called me. I wouldn't have wanted to miss this."

In spite of what he'd thought about Hadley earlier, he suddenly realized his attraction to her wasn't going to go away merely because he wanted it to.

Chapter 3

Hadley had amazed Eli as she'd helped deliver the foal. In spite of being short and slender, she *was* strong, and she was capable. As they'd tended the mare, they'd been huddled close. Very close. If he had leaned in, he could have kissed her.

But the enormity of the birth had prevented him from doing that. Watching the miracle had kept him grounded—grounded in what he did for a living, grounded in the satisfaction of raising horses, grounded in the knowledge that Hadley was an expert in her field.

As they sipped their coffee on stools,

watching momma and foal rest, he asked, "Where did you go to school?"

"Colorado State. It was a good experience."

"Have you been in Bozeman since vet school?"

"I have. They've been good to me at the practice. There are three vets, so we rotate and we can each get time off. That's how I was able to come here to Rust Creek Falls for Thanksgiving."

"Delivering a foal came back to you. Maybe you should expand your practice," he suggested.

She looked over at the colt. "Actually, doing this has revved up my interest in larger animals again. One of our vets specializes in farm and ranch animals. I might tag along with him more often."

She gestured to the lid that had come from the cookie jar. "I noticed those organic cookies for the horses."

"I try to keep up with the healthiest feeds and herbs that help temperaments. I keep everything as natural as possible," he confirmed.

"You use herbs for temperament?" she asked.

He nodded. "I mix them in with the feed. I've picked up a thing or two over the years."

He wasn't sure why he'd just made himself sound a lot older than she was. But he didn't think he was. He was thirty-five.

"How old are you?" Eli asked her.

"Thirty-one. Why?"

He shrugged. "I just wondered."

She narrowed her eyes. "Did you think I was younger or older than that?"

Releasing a long breath, he knew he'd backed himself into that corner. "I plead the fifth. No matter what I say, it will be wrong."

She laughed, and he liked the sound of her laughter.

Suddenly their attention was taken by Amber. Apparently the rest period for the mare was over. She stood and the umbilical cord broke.

Hadley quickly stood, too, as did he.

Arm to arm, they watched as the foal, on shaky legs, rose to its feet. Again, Eli could almost feel Hadley's emotions as she watched mother and baby bond.

Sometimes in the past, he'd had to guide the foal to its mom's nipple. But this foal found it easily. His momma nudged him a little and accepted him.

Eli knew they weren't out of the woods yet. The placenta still had to be delivered. If that didn't happen in about four hours, the risk of infection in the mare was greater. Once again he was glad that Hadley was here. Standing close together, shoulder to shoulder, arm to arm, he was disturbed by an attraction to Hadley that he now had to acknowledge.

But acknowledging it didn't mean he was accepting it. He stepped away. "I'm going to see what's going on outside."

He felt Hadley's gaze on his back when he went to the barn door. To his dismay, he couldn't get it open.

Hadley glanced his way. "What's the matter?"

Instead of going to the back door near the tack room this time, he went to the bigger door and tried to slide it on its tracks. He managed only a few inches when snow fell in. Lots of snow.

"We're snowed in," he announced.

Hadley came hurrying to the door, looked outside and gasped. "There has to be twenty inches out there."

"Close to it," he agreed, accepting the situation for what it was. After all, he did live in Montana.

Hadley began pushing some of the snow away. She looked almost frantic.

"What are you doing?"

"I have to get out. It's still snowing. There will be even more in a little while. I'll never be able to get back tonight."

Earlier, she'd sounded reconciled to the fact that she'd be here awhile. But maybe she hadn't considered an overnight stay. Was she panicked *because* of their attraction?

"Would that be so awful?" he teased, hoping to ease her anxiety.

Then he saw a multitude of emotions flash through her eyes. Panic. Maybe even a little fear. What was *that* about?

"I can't be cooped up with you," she said, kicking at the snow again but only managing to have it stick to her jeans and her boots.

He wasn't sure what made him do it, but he took her by the shoulders and turned her toward him. "Hey! You've got to relax. I have power bars stowed away in the tack room, peanut butter, canned stew and bottled water. As you said earlier, we have more than some people."

Just then, the lights in the barn blinked out.

"Oh, no," she said. "The electricity."

To reassure her, he gave her shoulders a

little squeeze. "The space heater is run by gas, and I have battery-powered lanterns. Not to mention a butane stove to warm the stew. We're not going to freeze or go hungry. This could be one of those times when you have to roll with the punches."

"Oh, I've rolled with plenty of punches," she insisted, looking almost angry about it. She jerkily pulled away from him.

He couldn't understand her withdrawal and couldn't help but take it personally. Apparently being cooped up with a cowboy wasn't her cup of coffee.

"Look," he said, "you don't have anything to fear from me. I'll be the perfect gentleman." He raised his hands in a surrender gesture. "I won't touch you. Promise."

Then he pushed the door to the outside world closed again before any more snow could fall in. When Hadley didn't say a word, he left her standing there as he returned to Amber and her foal.

Hadley stood in a far corner of the barn, cell phone in hand, trying to get a connection. She was upset with herself and upset with the situation. Eli wanted her to roll with the punches. She'd certainly done that in the past. But for some reason, it was harder to do it now.

She tried again to connect with Melba or her sister. But her texts wouldn't go through. She was glad she'd texted after she'd arrived. At least her family knew she was safe here.

Safe?

Oh, she was sure Eli would be the perfect gentleman because he said he would. From everything she knew about him he was steady, reliable and kept his word. Not only that, but from their conversation, she'd gleaned the fact that he wasn't narrow-minded like some cowboys. He seemed to have a wealth of knowledge about many subjects.

The bottom line was that she was attracted to him and didn't want to be. Worse, she was cooped up with him in an almost intimate situation. The birth of that foal had *made* this situation intimate. She'd felt it when the baby was born and she and Eli had gazed into each other's eyes. They both valued that momma and colt the same way. That had made Eli even more attractive to her. And when the colt had stood on wobbly legs and gone to his momma, she was so touched she could have cried.

Trying to get a grip on the situation, she

told herself she could handle her attraction to Eli. All she had to do was ignore it. She knew how disastrous instant attraction could be. She'd lived with the regrets that had come from it. Attraction had caused the biggest mistake of her life.

Still, she knew she'd offended Eli, and she needed to apologize. She just didn't know the best way to do it.

For a while, Eli had been closeted in the tack room, coming out now and then to check on Amber and her colt. Whenever he did, his face softened just looking at them. But as soon as he turned away, he was stoic again.

She had to fix this. They would be stuck here together until tomorrow. She'd accepted the situation for what it was—she was snowed in with Eli. But this awkwardness between them was her fault, and she had to remedy it.

Thinking about the best way to approach the sexy rancher, first she checked on the momma cat and kitten. The kitten was nursing, and its momma looked content. Hadley hoped they were both healthy. When she left, she'd take them to Brooks's clinic.

Noticing the tin of chocolate chip cookies, she remembered she and Eli had eaten only a few. They'd be delving into the rest for supper. She checked her watch, glowing in the darkness of the barn. It was almost suppertime. Eli had set one battery-powered lantern near Amber's stall and another in the tack room. He had a third he could carry wherever he went.

She glanced around the tack room. Eli had mentioned a butane-powered stove. Maybe they could warm water for hot tea. She always carried tea bags in her purse. It was a habit she'd started in college when she'd had a mug warmer in her room. She still carried that mug warmer in her SUV, but it wouldn't do any good if she couldn't plug it in. But a portable stove would be a means to mediation. She decided a peace offering might be the best way to start conversation again with Eli.

Rooting in her purse, she found the small plastic bag she kept the tea bags in. Taking her courage in hand, she walked to Amber's stall. Eli was sitting on a stool watching the mare. It was actually hard to see him because he wasn't right by the lantern.

He must have heard her footsteps because he turned toward her. "They seem to be doing well," he said in an even tone.

"Yes, they do," she agreed, not knowing how to begin. It seemed she was as bad at apologies as being cooped up with Eli. She wiggled the plastic bag in her hand. "I have a few tea bags. I thought maybe we could warm water on the stove. Even weak tea would be something to warm us up."

He studied her in the shadows. She noticed his jaw lose some of its rigidity, and his stance relaxed some. "Hot tea sounds good. I'll see if I can rustle up a pot to use."

She followed him to the tack room and watched as he took out the portable stove and fired it up. Then he opened the cupboard and dug around inside. He produced not only a small saucepan but canned beef stew. "When I spend time down here with an ailing horse, I make do with whatever supplies are around. How do you feel about beef stew from a can?"

"If we can warm it up, it will be great. If we can't, I'll leave the beef stew to you and I'll take the power bar."

Opening another upper cabinet, he took out the box of power bars. "We can sit in here for a spell. If you're cold, you can wrap up in a saddle blanket." He gestured to a man's suede jacket hanging on a peg behind the door. "Or put that on, on top of your coat."

"I'm fine," she assured him, imagining the

feel of Eli's coat around her, his scent enveloping her.

He handed her the saucepan. "If you want to start the water, I'll find a flashlight. We might need that, too. The lantern batteries could run out."

As Eli left the tack room, Hadley realized that he was a planner and apparently thought ahead, always prepared with plan B.

She set the water to boil and glanced over at the momma cat and kitten. They stayed cuddled together in the bed Eli had made.

When he returned to the tack room with two flashlights, Hadley said, "I'll have to feed momma again when we're done. She needs nourishment to be able to nurse her baby."

From somewhere Eli had found two more foam cups. Hadley dropped a tea bag into each. "I hope you like orange spice. That's all I have."

"Orange spice is fine. My mother has a whole cupboard full of everything from chamomile to Earl Grey."

Again Eli had surprised her. Men didn't usually notice that kind of thing. "You're a tea drinker?"

"It's not always my choice," he admitted. "But whenever Mom wants to talk, she pours us both a cup of tea. In a sense, I've learned what I like and what I don't."

From the cabinet he pulled out a jar of peanut butter. "We can always slather peanut butter on the cookies."

With a smile, she suggested, "I think beef stew and plain cookies will be fine."

Once the water for the tea was poured, Eli popped the top of the beef stew can and dumped it into the saucepan. He found a few utensils in a drawer and used a fork to stir the stew. The light from the lantern was bright in the dark room and played over Eli as he prepared their dinner.

She handed him a cup of tea. "It should be brewed. You don't want it to get cold."

"It will feel good going down."

Every time Eli spoke, his deep voice seemed to mesmerize her. She found herself staring at his face, the creases around his mouth, his firm jaw, his lips. She didn't know why, but she got the feeling that he was a sensual man, not afraid of touching.

She quickly shut down that thought and took a sip of her tea. It was hot and did feel good going down. Now was the time to apologize.

However, just as she was about to open

her mouth, and probably put her foot in it, he looked away, down at the stew. "I think it's ready," he said, and she wondered if he'd been studying her face as carefully as she'd been studying his.

He'd found only one bowl in the cupboard. It had a black stripe around the outer rim and was chipped here and there. "We'll have to eat out of the same bowl," he told her gruffly. "Or you can have the bowl and I'll eat out of the pot."

"Whatever suits you is fine with me." After all, she *could* roll with the punches, couldn't she?

After a quick glance at her, he said, "You take the bowl." He produced a glove from somewhere, and when he sat on the desk chair, he laid it on his thigh. Then he propped the pot on that.

They ate for a few minutes in companionable silence, hearing only the sounds of the wind against the barn, the soft whinnies of horses stirring in their stalls, the creak of the timbers overhead as the roof absorbed the cold.

Finally, she moved restlessly on the stool and worked up her nerve. "Eli, I'm sorry about earlier."

"Earlier?" he asked as if he didn't know what she was talking about.

"I never meant to give the impression that I thought—"

He cut in. "That you thought I was just a cowboy. That I only knew how to rope a steer. That I didn't pay attention in school because my life was only here on the ranch."

She wasn't sure what to say to all that.

As if he'd never intended to say what he had, he sighed and ran a hand through his thick hair. "I guess we all have preconceived notions."

She was cognizant of the fact that he didn't mention what his might be about her.

He did add, however, "Just so you know, I ran track. I could have had a scholarship to college."

"You didn't want to go?" There was no judgment in her voice. She seriously wanted to know.

"I had other things on my mind then. And, no, I didn't see the need. One year passed into two and then three. My parents depended on me, and I'd made a life here."

He wasn't saying what had happened in those years after high school, and she really had no right to pry. She certainly didn't want him asking *her* personal questions.

After Eli had finished his stew, he set the pan on the desk. Hadley passed him her bowl, and he set that on top of the pan. She couldn't help but slip her phone from her pocket and check it.

"There's still no signal," she said with disappointment.

"Your family knows you're here." His tone was reassuring.

She shook herself free of the notion that her family was worrying about her. "Old Gene and Melba know I can take care of myself. I don't think they'll worry. What about *your* parents?" she asked him.

"They'll have watched the weather reports for here from Missoula. They'll know what's happening. I've often handled the ranch on my own, and they know everything will be taken care of."

"Because you're the dependable one?" Hadley asked.

"Something like that," he said with a nod. "I'm the oldest, so I've probably always had more responsibilities than the others."

She could easily see that.

"Ready for that cookie now?" he asked

with a smile that made him look rakish and charming, even handsome. At first she'd thought his face was too craggy to be handsome, but she'd been wrong. And now with a bit of beard stubble shadowing his jaw, he was downright sexy. Way too sexy.

"A cookie sounds good," she said, noticing the husky tone in her voice. Eli Dalton made her insides quiver.

The cookie tin was sitting on the desk. Removing the lid, he smiled at her. "There's only one. Do you want it?"

"We can split it," she suggested.

He took it from the decorative tin, and she couldn't help but notice his long fingers and large hands. Those hands had been so gentle on Amber.

As if he'd caught her watching him, he said, "I washed up a bit ago. I let snow melt and added dish detergent."

"I wasn't thinking that—" Her voice broke off because she didn't want to tell him what she had been thinking. That the touch of his hand on her skin would be a pleasurable thing. She was hoping he couldn't see her blush in the dusky barn.

He didn't question her further. Rather, he broke the cookie in half and gave her the larger piece. That said something about him, too. Not only that he was a gentleman, but that he might often be self-sacrificing. No. She was reading too much into a simple gesture. No man she had ever known had been self-sacrificing, and certainly not the one she'd gotten entangled with.

"What's wrong?" Eli asked.

She took a bite of the cookie. "What makes you think something's wrong?"

"You were frowning. Not just a simple frown, but a deep one."

"Just thinking about something in the past I'd rather forget," she said truthfully, then finished the cookie and the rest of her tea. Her thoughts pushed her away from Eli. "I'm going to check on Amber."

Once she was on her feet, she didn't want to seem rude, so she asked, "Are you going to name the colt?"

"I'm going to wait until tomorrow so I can see him better in the light. I like to let the babies name themselves."

She liked that idea. In fact, she liked a lot about Eli Dalton.

Eli watched Hadley walk away with the third lantern, wondering what had unsettled her again. He took the empty cookie tin and the dirty pan to the counter. There he poured in the soapy mixture he'd made from the melting snow. That would have to do until morning or whenever someone plowed them out. That's what it was going to take. He could probably forge a path through to the house, though it would be foolish in a blizzard. If he'd been more prepared, he would have tied a length of rope from the door of the house to the barn as a guide rope. But there was really no reason why he and Hadley couldn't stay in the barn comfortably until morning. Then they could decide if they wanted to venture to the house.

He wondered if the snow was still coming down. He didn't want to attempt to open the door and have it get jammed in the snow, letting cold air in. But there was another way he and Hadley could check on the outside world to see what was happening.

When Eli returned to Amber's stall, Hadley was standing there watching momma and baby.

"This is a sight you can never get tired of," she said.

He felt that connection again with Hadley because she understood the bonds between mother and baby. "I know," he agreed. Then he said, "And I know another sight that's spectacular, too. Come with me to the hayloft." He picked up the lantern Hadley had carried to the stall.

She glanced over her shoulder at him. "Seriously?"

"I don't have a secret lair up there," he promised her. "I just want to show you something."

"Famous last words," she mumbled under her breath, and he had to grin. Just what kind of men had she been associating with?

"We'll have to feed the horses, and I want to make sure everything's locked up for the night first," he explained. "This will be the first step in doing that. Come on."

"Do I need to bring anything with me?" she asked, trailing after him.

"Nope. Just your sense of wonder."

When he stopped, turned around and studied her, he could see she had no idea what he meant. But she followed him, and that meant she trusted him...a little.

Making sure the loft ladder was steady, he asked, "Do you want me to go up first, or do you want to climb first?"

"You go first," she said. "You know where you're going."

Easily he climbed the ladder to the hayloft,

still holding the lantern. He was used to doing it. Once there, he waited for her.

She climbed up more slowly, careful each booted foot was steady as she took the next rung. As she reached the top of the ladder, he held out his hand. She hesitated only a moment, took it and held on until her feet were firmly planted in the hayloft and the straw there. Holding her hand like that, he felt more than a little warmth zing up his arm. But when she was balanced, she quickly let go.

She looked around, and he could tell she was trying to compute what he wanted to show her. Bales of hay and a few farm implements sparsely dotted the hayloft. He went to the doors. They were made like shutters, two halves coming together to form the door closing. Now he unlatched the left side and let it swing open. Then he did the same thing on the right. The snow had stopped for now, but the wind still blew. The sight beyond the barn was worth the frigid rush of air.

When he beckoned to Hadley, she stepped closer, finally realizing what he wanted her to see. Under the moon glow, the landscape was pristine, white as far as the eye could see. Fir trees rose up in the distance against a blue-black sky.

"What a view!" Hadley said with awe in her voice. "This is what Christmas dreams are made of."

"Or a cowboy's winter dream," Eli said softly. "The snow causes problems, that's for sure. It's going to take us a while to dig out. We'll even have to get the corral clear so we can exercise the horses. But I wouldn't give up moments like this to live anywhere else."

One moment they were standing in the straw looking out over the snow-covered landscape, and the next they were gazing at each other. Understanding seemed to pass between them once more, and something even more potent. Hadley's face was tilted up to his. He'd set the lantern on the floor a couple of feet away so it wouldn't ruin their view of the outside. He couldn't see much, but he could see the sparkle in her eyes, the look on her face that said maybe, just maybe, she was thinking the same thing he was—that a kiss right now could be something special. He wanted to reach for her, pull her close. But if he did and she didn't want that, or if he did and she suddenly got scared, they still had the rest of the night to spend together. He wanted her to trust him, and a kiss right now could end that possibility before it even started.

A cold gust of wind suddenly blew their way, and Hadley shivered. That was a signal.

He couldn't refrain from touching her, though, so he gently placed his hand on her shoulder. "Come on. I don't want you to get colder than you are. We can go back to the tack room and warm up. I just thought you needed a little entertainment tonight."

"That view is better than a movie," she assured him, turning toward the ladder.

After he secured the doors to the hayloft, he said, "Maybe I should go down the ladder first. I can make sure you don't fall."

"I can get around on my own quite well," she protested a bit defensively.

"All right," he said. "Go on. I'll follow you."

She gave him a look that was cautious, no doubt because he'd given in so easily. He watched as she tried to figure out how to maneuver herself over that top rung of the ladder from the hayloft. Finally, she got down on her knees and eased onto the first rung backward.

"Maybe I *should* have let you go first," she muttered.

"Hindsight is twenty-twenty," he said amiably.

In the light of the lantern, he could see her glare. Ignoring it, he held the ladder steady until she was halfway down. Then he maneuvered onto it and climbed down after her.

When he'd reached the barn floor, too, she said, "You mentioned we have to feed the horses. Any special feed for Amber?"

"It's made up in the bin next to the large one. It's a special mix that should suit her well for the next couple of weeks."

Apparently Hadley was going to help him. She easily found the bin, scooped the feed into a bucket and took it to Amber while he fed the other horses. When he passed the birthing stall, he told her, "I'll lay out blankets in the tack room. Hopefully that will be enough cushioning so we can sleep. Are you okay with that?"

"We can be thankful for the heater," she said, not expressing what she thought about the blankets.

Following the trend of her thoughts, he added, "And we can be thankful that we have friends and family out there who will see that we get dug out as soon as possible."

"And if we aren't dug out tomorrow?" Hadley asked in a low voice.

"If we're not dug out by noon, I'll get to the house somehow and figure out how to get you there, too."

But Hadley didn't look reassured by his words, just worried. "What if the snow starts again?"

"It has to stop sometime." He could see her eye roll from the light of the lantern he carried. He asked seriously, "Wouldn't you rather think about the best rather than the worst?"

"I would, but that doesn't mean the best is going to happen."

There was something about Hadley that told him she'd been through a crisis that had colored her view of men and maybe even the world. The question was—would she let him get to know her well enough to find out her secret?

Chapter 4

Hadley knew it made sense that she and Eli would bunk down together in the tack room/office where the heater was located. But the situation was still awkward. She'd be sleeping in here practically side to side with Eli! He'd gathered all the saddle blankets he could find, and now she helped him spread two of them across the floor. He'd found a sleeping bag tucked on a shelf. He'd unrolled that, opened it and laid it over the blankets.

Looking around the tack room instead of looking at him—because he drew her gaze to him much too often—she said, "This room looks a lot newer than the rest of the barn."

"This was an old barn, so we added on the tack room/office, and that other small room for tools. It works well. We don't have to worry about the heater causing condensation in the rest of the barn."

"And it keeps the moisture from your tack."

"Exactly." He went to the shelves again and produced an orthopedic pillow. "Dad uses this when his back's bothering him. You can have it for under your head."

"What about you?"

"I'll use my vest."

"Should I keep my coat on?"

"We'd be better off under a blanket letting our body heat combine. You can use your coat as an extra covering or under you for more padding."

Letting their body heats combine?

"Eli—" she protested almost breathlessly.

"Look. I know this isn't the ideal situation. But we're both going to have our clothes on. It's not as if this is a romantic overnight escapade."

No, it wasn't. But as she studied Eli, she knew it could be. Oh, not tonight. They'd both set boundaries. But he was a hunk and she was a red-blooded woman, though that red blood had turned cool over the past few years.

Yes, she'd told everybody she was too busy to date, but it was so much more than that.

"Do you need a power bar before we bunk down?" he asked.

"No, but we should check mom and foal at intervals."

"The heater's on a timer, and it will go on and off. That always wakes me. I'll make sure I check them."

"I can take my turn."

"No need if you're sleeping. But if you're awake, you're welcome to."

Eli had left a lantern switched on and placed it on the desk. Taking his jacket from the peg behind the door, he put it on, then carried the other lantern out into the barn to make one last check. She was sure he wasn't checking only momma and baby, but the other horses, too. The wind had picked up again. It buffeted the tack room addition as if it was trying to push it into the main part of the barn. But she knew the construction was solid. Anything the men in this family did would be solid.

While Eli was gone, she wandered around the tack room, running her hand over the leather saddles, realizing what good condition everything was in. Even the stirrups were clean. This family obviously knew how to run a ranch and keep it in good shape. Maybe she was just trying to distract herself because she didn't want to lie down on that floor and wait for Eli. That was too reminiscent of—

She put the thoughts out of her head.

When Eli returned to the tack room, his jacket looked wet. Melting snow shone on it by the light of his lantern.

"Did you try to go outside?" She looked down at his boots, and they were wet, too.

"*Try* is the operative word. About half of me got out the door. There's just no point even attempting it. The blowing snow is icy."

"Do you have snowshoes?" she asked, nervous because she couldn't imagine how they would ever make their way to the house if they had to.

"I have a pair, but they're up at the house. We have a snowmobile, too. Sometimes we need it to get out to the cattle. We'll have to take it all into consideration by noon tomorrow if no one's here to plow us out."

To distract herself from being snowbound with Eli, Hadley peered into the box where momma cat was sleeping, her baby tucked in beside her. She noted, "They don't seem the least bit perturbed about all this."

"You have to remember that they don't always know where their next meal's going to come from, at least momma cat doesn't. She takes food when she can find it. She takes comfort when she can find it."

Hadley thought about that. "I guess you're right. Cats live from moment to moment. Maybe we'd be better off if we did the same."

"We're trying to do that tonight," he suggested, looking at their makeshift bed. "Are you ready to call it a night? I have to wipe down my jacket, but go ahead and get settled. I'll be there in a minute."

By getting settled, she supposed he meant taking off her hat, jacket and boots. The jacket was first. She decided to lay it long ways under her to provide more comfort. The fleece would go only so far, but she'd take what she could get. She'd worn double socks inside her boots, so her feet shouldn't get too cold. Besides dressing for the cold, she really hadn't thought about what she was wearing when she'd driven out here today. So her jeans and a long-sleeved sweater in multiple shades of blue weren't exactly her best garments. But what did that matter anyway? She was going to be rolled up in blankets on the floor.

As Eli dried off his coat, he asked, "Any nighttime routines?"

"What? Like covering my face with a blue mask so nobody would recognize me, yet it would make me glow in the morning?"

He was quiet a few moments and she didn't know why, but apparently he'd been thinking over what he was going to say. "I can't imagine you'd need a blue mask to glow in the morning."

She was speechless. She was rarely speechless. "That's an awfully nice thing to say."

"It's not just nice, it's true. You have that kind of face. When that foal was born, you glowed like the sunrise. That's the way I picture you in the mornings."

To get the subject away from *her* and his words that made her almost breathless, she sat down on the floor on the bedroll they'd made and asked, "What's it like, living with extra guys in the house?"

"When a fire burned down Uncle Phil's house, he and his five sons weren't just looking for a new house, they were looking for a fresh start. They came here to regroup."

"So your uncle has five boys?"

"Yep. Zach, Garrett, Shawn, Booker and Cole. They sure filled up our house again.

I mean our family house," he added. "I'm just glad I got my place done so I'm out of the mix."

"You don't enjoy being with them?"

"They're all good guys, and yes, I like them. We can talk about ranching all day and all night. But I have more experience, and I guess I just look at life differently than they do. Take my brother Derek for instance. He's at one extreme. He wants to have fun every weekend, nights, too, if he's not too tired. Me, on the other hand, I look at the work—that comes first. I make sure I have that done, all of it, before stepping out. Zach, Garrett, Shawn, Booker and Cole are somewhere in between. But sometimes when I'm with them, I just feel a lot older, like I don't belong there."

"They make you feel that way?"

"Oh, no. They never would."

Eli set the lantern on the floor beside the bedroll and then lowered himself beside her. She hadn't covered up yet, but now she did. Yes, she had all her clothes on, but the blanket gave her another layer of protection.

In the next few moments, they settled themselves side by side with at least six inches between them. Silence wound about them like a web that was almost claustrophobic as they lay there. Hadley broke it by asking, "So do you think your uncle wants to buy a ranch around here?"

"He already has an eye on a place similar to the Stockton family property—Sunshine Farm—and he's looking into it. He and his sons like Rust Creek Falls. They like the way it made a comeback after the flood. It could have just disintegrated into nothing like some small towns do. But the people here really rallied, and volunteers came from everywhere to help. That's how Brooks Smith met Jazzy. She was one of those volunteers. They make a great couple. When you see them together, you just know they belong together."

"I agree with that. Their passion is their work," Hadley mused. "They have that in common."

Eli agreed. "What more could they ask for?"

"I think Jazzy wants a family," Hadley suggested.

"That will come."

Would it, Hadley wondered? The older a woman got, the harder it could be to get pregnant. That's what her sisters had been ribbing her about, and she knew there was some truth in it.

Thinking about that, she was hopeful she'd fall asleep, but during the first couple of hours of lying on the blanket bedside Eli, Hadley didn't sleep. She was aware of his breathing, his every movement. She tossed and turned, careful not to let her hand brush Eli's, not to let her arm nudge his. She stayed on her side and her side only. But in spite of the blankets and the sleeping bag, the floor was hard. In spite of the heater in the room, the air was still chilled. To her dismay, she began to shiver.

Eli must have heard her teeth chattering because he turned around to face her. "Are you cold?"

"Yes. And I'm thinking about tomorrow and how we're going to get out of here, and about the mare out there and the foal, and the other horses."

"And world peace, and if your family's worrying?" She heard his soft laughter.

"My mind doesn't want to turn off."

"I think it would if you got warm. Come here."

She could tell he'd held out his arm to her.

"Come on," he coaxed. "Combined body heat will warm you up."

She didn't know if she was being stupid to try it. But she *was* cold. And if she was going to get any sleep tonight, she had to warm up. She moved into the crook of Eli's arm, and he wrapped it around her.

"Better?"

Oh, yes, it was better. Too much better. Being this close to him sounded alarm bells in her mind because she was attracted to him. Taking a deep breath, she managed, "I am warmer."

"Good. Then don't move. Let's talk about something that isn't in your head or on your to-do list."

"Like?" she asked, wondering where he was going with this.

"Like...tell me your favorite building in the whole world."

It was an odd question, but she went along with it. "That depends on what it's used for, or whether we're looking at it just for architecture."

"All in all."

"Probably the Louvre in France. What's yours?"

"The Smithsonian Air and Space Museum. As a boy I wanted a piece of my own moon rock."

She laughed. "Did you go on camping trips, look up at the sky and learn the constellations?"

"Sure did. Whenever Mom could, she bought us books on our favorite subjects. One of mine was astronomy. Kristen liked the classics, plays mostly. They made her into the actress she is. What did you read about most as a kid?"

"Do you know the author Zane Grey?" Hadley asked.

"Of course I do. He lived in Arizona for a while, and wrote about Oak Creek Canyon."

"Exactly," she said. "One of the most beautiful places on the planet."

And so it went. Hadley soon realized Eli wasn't like most cowboys, or even like his dad. Charles Dalton was a man of few words. Eli could easily paint pictures with his words, especially of his antics with his brothers and sisters when they were young. That made her laugh. Before she knew it, she was comfortably snuggled into his shoulder and falling asleep.

When Eli awakened, he felt totally disconcerted. He was practically hugging Hadley, and her cheek was against his chest. They'd both been up several times during the night, checking on Amber and the foal. When one moved, the other knew it, so they hadn't taken turns, they'd just gotten up together. It had been intimate in an odd way, but not as intimate as the way they were tucked together now.

The last time they'd checked on the horses, it had been 4:00 a.m. Gazing up at the frosted window, he realized it was morning.

He reached for his phone that he'd laid beside their blankets. It was almost 9:00 a.m., much later than he'd ever slept.

Hadley stirred. As he studied her, he realized she was much more vulnerable asleep than awake. Awake, she always seemed to have her guard in place. He wondered whether it was just around him, and knew he had to resist the urge to find out.

However, when her eyes flew open and she looked up at him, her brown eyes stunning, her pretty face so tempting in the morning light, he couldn't help but lean closer to her.

"We overslept," he murmured. "It's almost nine."

The momma cat and kitten were curled up and sleeping, snug against Hadley's hip. She couldn't move and didn't seem to want to.

"We have to feed the horses," she said, but she still gazed up at him.

"We do," he agreed. He didn't move either. It was as if they were being drawn together by a magnetic force, one stronger than he'd ever felt before. He could see in her eyes that she felt it, too. Their body heat had kept them warm throughout the night. Now he felt as if a furnace had been turned on high in the room.

"Hadley..." he said, and leaned in even closer so she'd realize his intent.

She gave a little sigh, lifted her chin a notch and waited. If she'd given any indication she didn't want him to kiss her, he would have thrown off the blanket and rushed into the barn. But her lips parted slightly, and he decided real time and the real world didn't mean much right now. They were closeted in their own world where the only thing that mattered was their attraction to each other.

Eli was taken by surprise when his lips brushed Hadley's. Just from that simple touch there was heat and a potent desire he didn't know if he'd ever felt before. He didn't know what he'd intended, but he got more than he bargained for. When his tongue swept her bottom lip, she responded. Her hand went to his neck, her fingers tunneling in the hair at his nape. His arm curved around her tighter. As his tongue touched hers, sparks became a roaring fire. He slanted his mouth to gain better access. His tongue darted against hers, probing and stroking. She gave as good as he did.

He wasn't thinking. He was only feeling, sensation after sensation, when a noise punctured the sensual haze that surrounded them. He couldn't make sense of it at first because all of his attention was on this amazing kiss. But then the hum became a growl and then a churning, and he realized someone from the outside world was coming to their rescue.

The only problem was, he didn't know if he wanted to *be* rescued.

Either his break in concentration affected Hadley, or she, too, was aware of the noise coming from what had to be a snowplow.

"I guess we'd better—" She started to sit up.

"I'd better open the door so they know we're in here," he said.

And before Eli knew it, they'd scrambled apart and gotten to their feet. Hadley scooped up the kitten, folded her into the crook of her arm, and was petting her as if her life depended on it.

When he was unsettled like this, the way he handled it was by action. So he said, "I'll go meet them," though he didn't know who "them" was. All he knew was that whoever was running those snowplows had saved him and Hadley from either a mistake or a terribly awkward situation. What had led him to kiss her like that?

He was still asking himself the question when he shoved his arms into his jacket and wrenched the door open so hard, the wood squealed. But he still couldn't push it open more than six inches. He'd left his Stetson on a peg near the door. Now he grabbed it, pushed it through the opening and waved it outside. They should see a black hat against all that white snow.

And they did. As he watched, he recognized Old Gene running the snowplow. Hadley's grandfather drove the machine practically up to the door. Levi Wyatt, Hadley's sister Claire's husband, jumped down from the other side of the snowplow with a shovel in his hand. Gene could get only so close to the door, but Levi soon shoveled a path the rest of the way so Eli could push the door open.

Behind him, Eli was aware of Hadley. She'd come out of the tack room and shut the door, probably to keep the kitten and her momma inside. Knowing her, she'd probably fed them, too.

Soon both Gene and Levi were in the barn checking on them.

"So I see the two of you survived," Old Gene said, as he first looked at Eli and then at Hadley.

"Amber had her foal," Hadley said in way of explanation. "Momma and colt are doing just fine. I want to help Eli feed the horses before I get out of here, and I have to take the momma cat and kitten along. Can I get around anywhere in town?"

Levi gave her an odd look, as if he knew she didn't spend most nights in a barn with a practical stranger. "Main Street in town has been cleared. Some plows are working on the side streets."

Gene seconded that with a nod. "You should be able to get to the clinic and back to the rooming house."

"You don't have to help me feed the horses," Eli said. "I know you want to get going."

"It will take me a few minutes to shovel out her car," Levi said. "So you don't have to rush if you want to make sure everything's okay in here before you leave."

"I'll find you a box for the cat and kitten," Eli told her. Without meeting her gaze, he went to do just that.

He needed time to think, time to remember, time to figure out exactly how Hadley Strickland had mixed up his thoughts and his feelings until he didn't know which way was up.

As soon as Hadley was closer to town, she phoned Brooks. To her surprise, he was at the clinic. "I stayed overnight," he said. "We had a couple of patients I wanted to make sure were okay."

"Jazzy was alone at the ranch?" She thought about the horses there as well as his dad, who still needed care.

"A part-timer who helps with the horses stayed with Jazzy overnight. My wife is quite capable, you know."

"I know," Hadley admitted. "It's just with the blizzard and the electricity out, it's tough to be alone on a night like that."

"I talked to her this morning, and everything's fine at the ranch. Where are you?"

"Since you're at the clinic, I'm on the way to you. I have a momma cat and a baby who have to be checked out and tested. They were in Eli's barn."

"So you were there overnight?" His voice held more than that simple question.

"I was. The mare and foal are doing well, and Old Gene and Levi came to plow us out. I'll be at the clinic in about five minutes."

And she was. She was able to park along the street but had to climb over a snowbank holding the box with the cat and kitten. Brooks must have seen her coming though because he came out and took the box. Everywhere she looked she saw mountains of snow. The street was cleared, and the walk around the clinic was shoveled or snow blown. She was sure Brooks had taken care of that.

Once inside the clinic, Brooks said, "Let's get these two tested, then we'll see what else we can do for them." Brooks took them into an exam room, and she stayed with them as he got the samples he needed.

While she was with her own furry clients in Bozeman, she tried to keep busy waiting for test results. But here, all she could do was pet the two cats and think about Eli. Not only think about Eli, but think about that kiss. She supposed it was natural when two people were attracted to each other—and they certainly were—for something like that to happen. They'd been in close contact for hours, sleeping cuddled together for body heat. The attraction had just suddenly walloped them both. At least she guessed that's what had happened. She'd protected herself so carefully for so long, never letting her guard down, never letting an attraction take over again. But yesterday, watching the birth, finding the cat and kitten, being cooped up in that room with Eli, somehow she'd become vulnerable again. She couldn't let that happen. She really couldn't.

When Brooks returned to the exam room, he was smiling. He was an attractive man, over six foot. He was lean and broad-shouldered with dark brown eyes that usually had a twinkle. But nothing about him made her heart go pitter-patter. Nothing about him attracted her the way Eli did.

"What's the verdict?" she asked, and realized she was holding her breath.

"They're clear, both FIV and feline leukemia. But I agree that the kitten could use eyedrops. And they both need a flea treatment. Is Eli going to keep them? The baby requires more care than running around a barn."

"I don't know what he'll do. I suppose I

could call him. Maybe since we're not in the midst of a blizzard, I can reach his cell."

Brooks must have noticed her tentative tone because he asked, "Didn't you two get acquainted while you were there?"

"We were caring for the horses," she said, almost defensively.

Brooks's eyebrows arched. "I didn't mean to suggest otherwise, but you must have had time to talk. You're a good judge of character. You know how to take care of human clients as well as the furry ones. Didn't you get a read on Eli?"

Oh, she'd gotten a read on him okay. At least she thought she had. But then really, what could you get to know in just a few hours?

"I like the way he handled his horse," she answered, noncommittally. "But I'll give him a call and see what he wants to do about the cats."

Brooks gave her an odd look and then a nod as he left the exam room.

She took out her phone. Eli answered on the second ring.

"Hadley," he said. "You got back to the clinic okay?"

There was that protective note again. She wasn't sure if it bothered her or reassured her.

"Yes. Brooks was here. He tested the cat and kitten, and they're clear of FIV and feline leukemia. But the little one needs eyedrops. I guess I'm calling to find out what you're going to do with them. You can't really let the kitten just run around loose in the barn."

"I suppose I could keep them in the office in the barn."

She thought about it. "You really should do that until the flea treatment works."

"Flea treatment?"

"Even in winter they can have fleas and ear mites. I'll give them a treatment that will take care of that, but you really need to give it forty-eight hours. You don't want to drag the fleas somewhere else."

"No, I certainly don't. Okay, in the office it is."

"Are you going to come pick them up?"

"I can do that. How long will you be there?"

Brooks could show Eli what to do, but she knew he probably wanted to get back to his ranch, too. "I can stay until you get here."

"I've been shoveling and snowblowing since the lane was opened. I'll take a break from that and come get them. I should be there in about fifteen minutes."

"See you then."

As the call ended, Hadley stared at her phone. She wondered if seeing Eli again would be an awkward reunion.

The kitten meowed, breaking into her thoughts, and she cuddled it next to her body. But her thoughts returned to the one subject that had dominated her mind for the last hour: Eli's kiss.

The best kiss of her life.

Chapter 5

Hadley heard the door to the clinic open and close. In the exam room with the momma cat and kitten, she waited for the knock on the door. It came.

Brooks opened the door a crack in case the cats were exploring on the floor. He immediately noticed she had kept them on a blanket on the table. "Eli's here," he said with a grin.

She supposed Brooks was just being his cheery self and she tried not to read anything into that grin.

Eli must have been right behind him because Brooks stepped aside and there the rancher was. He seemed even taller and more broad-shouldered in the exam room than he had in the barn. It made sense, she supposed. The exam room was smaller than the tack room. She always used logic when she was disconcerted or unsettled.

"I'm sorry to bring you out in this snowy mess," she apologized. "I didn't want to coop them up in a crate here if I didn't have to."

"No problem." When Eli came closer to the table, she felt a few sparks lighting her nerve endings. Maybe they came from remembering his hand on her face, the touch of his long fingers, the sensuality of his kiss. The room was getting warmer, and that wouldn't do at all.

"You said they tested clear?" he inquired, but his gaze was on her, not on the cats.

"They did." The kitten stood up when she saw Eli as if she remembered him.

She scrambled over to him, meowing, and he picked her up. "You're going to have to stay in the tack room for a day or two," he told her. He looked at Hadley. "Momma cat, too?"

"You'd better. Do you have any other cats around the barn?"

"I haven't seen any others. My guess is with this snow, none will go wandering either."

"Are you going to leave these two in the barn permanently?" She was having a problem keeping her mind on the conversation when Eli's gaze was locked on hers.

"I haven't decided yet. Maybe Mom will want them up at the house."

"Is she a cat person?"

"We've always had cats around the place. I just imagine Dad with a big bloodhound sitting by his side on the porch if he retires. But I don't think he'd like that picture."

"Probably not," she agreed. From everything she'd heard about Charles Dalton, he'd be active on the ranch until the day he died.

Why couldn't she stop looking at Eli? His gaze seemed to tether to hers. Trying to shake off the pull she felt toward him, she grasped at the nearest thing. The eyedrops. She held them tightly in her hand. "These are the eyedrops for the kitten. I thought we could give her the first dose together," she explained, covering up her nervousness. "Two hands are always better than one, so if you could get someone on the ranch to help you, that would be great. You'll have to give her the drops twice a day."

She showed him the small bottle and pointed to the instructions. "Just squeeze one drop into each eye. I'll hold her while you manage the bottle to see how fast the drops flow out."

"I have a feeling you're going to make this look easy when it's not."

"It *is* easy...once you do it a few hundred times."

He chuckled. "All right. I'm ready. I suppose the object of this is to do it quickly so she doesn't squirm away."

"Exactly." As she held the kitten, Eli let the drop fall into first one eye then the other. The kitten meowed loudly in protest. As soon as Hadley set her down on the table once more, she ran to her momma.

Eli ran his hand down the momma cat, and again Hadley noticed the gentleness of his touch, the way he brushed his fingers through the cat's fur. This time she grabbed a package from the counter and showed it to Eli. "These are a snack that will boost their immune systems. Give momma about ten each day. Baby can have two or three. Break them up for her."

"I'll take good care of these two," he assured her.

Hadley gave him a long look. He might want to take care of them, but he was a busy rancher, and she wondered if he'd forget them.

Apparently Hadley didn't hide her doubt. "I really will," he said again. "I just have to figure out the best way to do it."

He was about to pick up the box that she'd carried the cats in, but Hadley stopped him. "We have cardboard temporary carriers here. Let me get one of those for you. It will be much easier that way. The handles lock together, and you won't have to worry about the cats getting out."

Before she reentered the exam room a few minutes later, she took a deep breath. After she opened the door, she noticed that Eli was studying a chart on the wall while he carried the kitten in the crook of his arm.

He turned toward her. "You seem to be at home here."

"I've helped Brooks out a few times, so I know where things are."

"Since the receptionist isn't at the desk, should I pay you?"

Anne Lattimore, Brooks's receptionist, was snowed in. She'd called him and said she'd get here as soon as she could. But as far as Eli paying Hadley...

"Don't worry about paying today. Brooks will bill you for this office visit and the testing."

"You made an overnight house call, so I expect to pay you for your time, too."

"I was doing a favor for a friend. It was *my* time. I'm not going to charge for it."

"Hadley—" His voice was a husky, low protest.

She tried to ignore the way his voice seemed sensual and...intimate.

"Seriously, Eli. All I did was supervise."

"And probably save the colt," he concluded. "I named him Coco, by the way, because of his color."

In spite of her resolve not to fall under any man's spell ever again, she took a few steps closer to him. "It was an experience I won't soon forget."

They gazed into each other's eyes, knowing the birth of the colt had been the beginning of something else. However, Hadley didn't want to acknowledge that. Needing to keep her hands busy, she broke eye contact and opened the carrier on the table. Then she scooped up momma and set her inside. When Eli did the same with the kitten, his hand brushed hers. They looked at each other again as if not knowing what to say.

He closed the carrier and then picked it

up, hesitating only a second before going to the door.

Hadley walked him out to the reception area.

There he said, "I guess I'll see you around."

Hadley nodded but suddenly couldn't respond. Seeing Eli again would be a pleasure. But that was a pleasure she was going to deny herself.

When Hadley returned to the boarding-house from the clinic, she was met with hugs and kisses.

"Are you all right?" her grandmother asked.

"Did you freeze while you were out there?" her sister Claire inquired, looking her over.

"You'll have to tell us all about it," Old Gene suggested with a wink.

Hadley ignored that wink. Realizing she'd had little sleep and the adrenaline that had rushed through her when she was around Eli was ebbing, she was suddenly very tired. Oh, she'd gotten a few hours of sleep last night in Eli's arms. But the rest of yesterday and this morning had been exhausting, and she didn't think she was ready to face this crowd of family inquisitors.

Her sister Claire must have seen that because she said to the group, "Why don't we let Hadley get her bearings, change clothes, maybe even rest a bit. Then she can come down and have a snack with all of us."

While Melba and Old Gene seemed to agree, and Levi tended to his and Claire's daughter, Bekka, Claire spirited Hadley away up the stairs to the room where she was staying.

Once inside, Hadley flopped on the bed and said, "Thank you."

She sat there for a few seconds until Claire asked, "Well?"

"Well, what?"

"Well, aren't you going to tell me what happened?"

"Nothing happened. I delivered a foal. End of story."

"I hardly think so," her sister asserted. "I know what Eli Dalton looks like. He's hot."

Hadley kept silent.

"Not only is he hot, but you were cooped up with him for hours, and not only for hours, but overnight. Are you going to tell me again that nothing happened?"

The *nothing* that had happened had been a very surprising kiss. The other *nothing* that had happened had been her cuddling in Eli's arms. But she wasn't about to reveal either of those to Claire, just as she wasn't going to reveal what had happened in Las Vegas three years ago.

"Nothing happened," she said again, trying to make her sister believe it. "Eli felt the birth wasn't going right. That's why he called Brooks and Brooks called me. So I went out there. At first nothing seemed amiss, but as the mare began to deliver, we saw it was a breech birth. I had to give it a little assistance. We had a lot of time waiting around, and then being snowed in. We couldn't even get the barn doors open, not until we were plowed out this morning."

Claire gave her a long, level look. "I think you're leaving something out."

This was her sister after all, so Hadley grudgingly gave her something. "I will admit, Eli Dalton isn't what I expected. He's different from other cowboys I've met."

"How so?"

"He's self-taught, but knowledgeable in many subjects. He has a wide range of ideas. He doesn't seem mired just in his own thoughts or in a narrow point of view."

"Like other cowboys you've met?"

"Right."

"And just how many cowboys have you dated?"

Hadley shrugged. "A few."

"There's something you're *not* telling me. There's something that's kept you from seriously dating for a very long time. Don't you think you should spill what that is?"

Claire had this fine habit of making Hadley feel guilty. Yet Hadley knew once she let the cat out of the bag, so to speak, she could never live down her impulsive mistake. Her family would pounce on it. They'd want to fix it. They'd want to fix *her*. They'd want to hook her up with somebody eligible so she could settle down and begin the life they wanted for her.

But she wasn't exactly sure of the life she wanted. She didn't want to be poked or pressured or coddled...or looked at as a foolish woman who'd leaped into a situation without using her head. She just wanted to be treated like a normal woman who was finding her way.

"Claire, I'm fine. I have nothing to say. Everybody's dating habits are unique."

"Are you going to date Eli Dalton?"

"No. The subject never came up." Just because when they touched, she tingled. Just because when he kissed her, she swooned. Just because his gaze on hers made her feel like melting... No, the subject had never come up.

"There is something I didn't tell you," Hadley revealed.

Claire was all wide eyes and smiles now.

"I found a momma cat and kitten. I took them to the clinic and had them cared for, and Eli took them back home with him. The Circle D now has a momma and kitten as residents."

Claire swatted Hadley's arm. "Go get a shower and change. I'll pave the way for you downstairs and tell everybody that nothing happened."

"Thank you," Hadley said sweetly as she went to the shower. She knew Claire was frustrated with her, but she also knew as sisters they'd get through the frustrations. When Hadley returned to Bozeman in less than two weeks, she would no longer have to worry about spilling a secret she didn't want her family to know.

"I always thought Hadley Strickland was kind of standoffish."

Eli loved his brother Derek. He even liked him most of the time. But maybe not right now. They were sitting in the kitchen of their family home on Wednesday since the house was closer than his cabin. He'd just stopped in for a mug of coffee to warm him up before he continued checking fence lines that might have been damaged with the snow. Derek had come in about the same time.

"What do you mean she's standoffish?" Eli asked. "How do you even know her?"

"I've chatted her up," Derek admitted. "Weddings are a good place for that," he said with a wink. "But she acted all guarded, like I'd stepped on her toes or something."

"Did you try to ask her out without even having a conversation first?"

Derek gave a little shrug and a wicked grin. "Maybe."

His brother thought he could pretty much date any woman he wanted. Therefore, he figured there must be something wrong with Hadley if she wasn't interested in him.

"She's a smart woman, bro. She probably saw through your…charm."

Eli could see Derek was about to protest.

The truth was, he himself had seen a reserve around Hadley. In his experience, that kind of reserve usually came from having been hurt in a past relationship. In spite of himself, he wanted to know more about Hadley's past relationships, and more about the woman herself.

His past serious relationship had affected *him*. Out of high school, he and Elaine had dated for two years. Two years where he'd had dreams of owning his own ranch someday, building up a herd, having a family. But she'd broken his heart because she'd wanted a career in Chicago. She'd expected him to leave the ranch where he'd grown up, leave his family, friends and his heritage. He'd known then she'd never have the time and space in her life for what was important to him. He'd ended the relationship. That was the only thing he could have done.

That had been twelve years ago. Oh, sure, he'd dated since then, but not seriously. Never seriously.

In a flurry of movement, his mother came into the kitchen. She was plump with gray curly hair that framed her face. Spry and energetic, she always had something planned for her day. Today he saw baking pans were greased and floured on the counter. He also noticed that she'd set out a couple of pie plates. That gave him an idea.

She came over and gave him a hug. "I

haven't seen you for a couple of days. Where have you been keeping yourself?"

"There was lots of snow to shovel, and I had to make sure the cattle had feed."

"I suppose you did," she said, going to the sink and washing her hands. "But I also heard that you have a cat and kitten living at your place. What's that about?"

"They were living in the barn office, but since I have to put eyedrops in the kitten's eyes, it seemed best to keep them at my cabin."

His mother arched a brow. "Permanently?"

"I don't know yet."

Derek cut a glance his way, then went to the refrigerator for the carton of milk.

"Are you baking pies today?" Eli asked his mother.

"Probably tomorrow morning. I'm baking a couple of cakes today. With Thanksgiving coming, we'll need those cakes and I can freeze them. And the pies… I imagine everyone here will lay into them as fast as I bake them. It's just a matter of what you want—apple, pumpkin, chocolate cream?"

Eli didn't care what pies his mother made. They were all good. "Do you think you'll have an extra?"

She picked up the flour canister and brought it to the counter. "You want to take one to your cabin?"

"No. It's a thank-you present for Hadley Strickland. She wouldn't take any money for helping with Amber. I thought a pie might be a nice gesture."

Now his mother gave him the same probing look that Derek was giving him. "I suppose it could be. What kind do you want to take her?"

"Apple would do just fine."

His mother gave a nod. "Your favorite, too. That's convenient if you want to share."

Eli could say he would or wouldn't. On the other hand, he considered the best thing to do in this situation was just keep his mouth shut.

The next afternoon, carrying the basket his mother had insisted he use to hold the pie, Eli went to the door of Strickland's Boardinghouse. A minute or so after he knocked, Melba herself came to the door.

When she saw him, she was all smiles. "Hello, Eli. It's good to see you. I thought I might have a stray guest coming in for the holidays."

"From what I hear, you have a houseful of family."

"Yes, I do, and it's wonderful. What have you got there in the basket?"

"This is a thank-you gift for Hadley. Is she here?"

"She's up in her room with that e-reader of hers, reading veterinary journals." She shook her head. "I thought this would be a vacation for her."

"That's why I particularly want to thank her. She cut into her downtime to help me out."

"Come on in out of the cold," Melba invited, motioning him inside. "I'll go get her."

Eli felt a bit ridiculous standing in the foyer with the basket until Hadley came running down the stairs. Then he didn't much care how he looked. She was dressed in black leggings and an oversize blue-and-black tunic sweater. Although it was roomy, it hugged her when she moved. He had to smile at the furry slippers with embroidered paw prints.

When she saw him glance at her slippers, she said, "What can I say? I have a pet theme going on."

As she approached him, he felt as if he needed to rid himself of his coat. Instead he held the basket out to her. "That's an apple cranberry pie to thank you for your help. I wish I could say I baked it, but that was my mother's doing."

Hadley smiled at him. "So is the pie from you or your mother?"

"Oh, it's from me, and Amber."

Just then Bekka, Claire and Levi's three-year-old, came running into the foyer and threw her arms around Hadley's legs. Afterward, she turned and headed for the kitchen, where Eli could hear babies crying. He supposed they were Tessa and Carson's twin babies.

"Things are a bit noisy here," Hadley told Eli with a smile. "That's why I was in my room."

"Do you want to take a walk so we can talk?" he asked. He hadn't intended the invitation to spill out, but it seemed like a good idea.

"Sure. Just let me take the pie to the kitchen and I'll grab my boots and coat."

He couldn't tell from Hadley's expression if she was glad to see him or if the stroll would be anything more than a walk down the street. Just what did he expect from the walk except frostbite?

He was still contemplating that when Hadley met him at the door. After they went outside, she pulled gloves from her pockets and slipped them onto her hands. At the base of the steps, she asked, "East or west?"

"Let's go west. It looks as if the sidewalk's completely clear that way."

Some of the mounds along the curb were four feet high, but the pavement cut a swath through the snow that was just wide enough for the two of them to walk. Their arms brushed as they breathed in the cold and walked half a block in silence.

Finally, Eli broke it, knowing exactly what he'd expected from this walk. "We should talk about that kiss."

After a few footsteps, she cut a glance at him and asked, "You mean at least three kisses, don't you?"

He wasn't going to quibble. He thought about it as one long kiss, but they had come up for air twice.

"I see you're a detail person," he teased, not feeling as light as he sounded.

Her boots crunched on snow that had fallen from the mounds alongside the walk. "It was the situation we were in," she claimed. "That's all. I mean, haven't you kissed someone before because you were excited or relieved or…"

She seemed to run out of words, and he filled in for her. "Or very attracted to them?"

When he turned toward her, she looked troubled. Just what was going through her head? What held her back from telling him what she was feeling? Something was. He knew it in his gut.

He was absolutely certain of it when she suddenly changed the subject. "Has your household returned to normal? Everyone back safely from Missoula?"

So she wasn't going to talk about their attraction. He'd try again later. "They're all back. With cousins helping out, the workload is lighter. It's what I like most about ranching—the teamwork."

"Teamwork," she repeated. "I've mostly flown solo."

"But you said you cover for the other vets."

"I do. But the truth is, I have more of a relationship with my furry patients than with the other veterinarians."

"That's telling," Eli said before he thought better of it.

"Telling about what?" Hadley asked defensively.

Just because she wasn't going to be open with him didn't mean he couldn't be open with her. "I think that says you believe you don't need anyone else and no one else needs you."

She vehemently shook her head. "That's not true. My sisters count on me."

"But do you count on them?" he asked.

She went silent.

He stopped and faced her. "Hadley, I didn't mean that as criticism. Self-sufficiency is a wonderful thing. But now and then it's okay to admit you need somebody, don't you think?"

"I think *you* think we know each other better than we do."

He realized immediately she was distancing herself again. "Two people confined together for a day can get to know a lot about each other."

She didn't dispute that as they came to the end of the street. But he could see she didn't move to cross either way. So he turned to face her. "What are you afraid of, Hadley?"

It was probably the wrong thing to say because her shoulders squared, her chin went up and there was fire in her eyes. "I'm not afraid of anything."

She was full of bravado, but he didn't think it had any substance behind it. "And you believe that kiss was just about being thrown together unexpectedly."

"Sure. I mean— You're a sexy guy, Eli."

"And you're a sexy woman, Hadley."

She looked startled for a moment as if she might not believe him. He took advantage of her surprise. "But you don't want to talk about any attraction between us."

She blinked. "No, I don't. There isn't one. I mean, there's nothing between us."

He gave her a long probing look, then he took a step closer to her. "No attraction between us?"

She had that deer-in-the-headlights look, and he almost felt sorry that he was trying to prove a point. But he wanted to know what made Hadley tick. He wanted to know why she wouldn't admit to the attraction.

As he leaned a little closer, she sucked in a breath. The cold air must have shaken her back to reality because she said, "I have to get back to the boardinghouse. I'm going to babysit Bekka this afternoon while Claire runs errands."

"And the others won't be around?"

She shrugged. "Everybody has something to do."

She'd turned back toward the boardinghouse and he did, too, walking beside her once more. "Do you like kids?"

"Sure I like kids. I'm just not as aware of my biological clock ticking as some women. And my sisters, my grandmother and even my mother don't understand that."

"You have a lot you want to do and see," he suggested, feeling a sinking sensation in his stomach.

"Exactly. Once I get my pilot's license, all sorts of opportunities might open up for me."

"And you don't want to be tied down."

She looked him directly in the eyes. "No, I don't."

Though she said the words, and she said them with some vehemence, he didn't quite believe her. Yet he knew from experience that a woman with dreams and goals like Hadley had would bring only heartbreak to a man like him.

They walked until they reached the steps to the boardinghouse. There Eli said, "Enjoy the pie."

"I will. Thank you for bringing it, and thank your mom, too."

That crazy devil inside his head made him say, "You can thank her yourself sometime. You're always welcome at the Circle D."

Hadley looked as if she wanted to respond, but she didn't. She just gave him a fake smile, a wave and went up the steps and inside.

Eli felt as if more than the door to the boardinghouse had closed behind Hadley. She'd built a fence around herself with no gate. It was obvious she wasn't letting any man jump over that fence into her corral.

The night they'd spent together and that kiss were now only shadows from the past.

Chapter 6

The following day, Eli was grooming a bay gelding when he heard the barn door open and someone called, "Hello? Eli?"

"Over here," he called back, surprised to hear Hadley's voice.

She came down the walkway to him and said, "Derek told me you were in here."

"I'm surprised to see you," Eli said honestly.

"The pie was delicious. I was going to write your mom a note, then I thought I'd just come by and check on Amber and Coco."

Write his mom a note? Did anybody do that anymore? Apparently Hadley had some of the old-fashioned girl in her.

"Maybe the momma and the kitten, too," Hadley added, looking around the barn toward the tack room.

"I took the cats to my cabin," he explained. "That seemed better than leaving them alone in here. And there's too much activity at the main house. I was afraid they'd get scared and confused. When I went online and checked cat care and kittens, I read they do better in a confined space with someone around."

"You're right about that," she agreed, looking impressed.

"You can come over to my cabin and check them out after you examine Amber and Coco."

For a moment he thought he saw a panicked look in Hadley's eyes, as if that wasn't what she'd expected at all. But then she seemed to bolster herself and put on her most professional voice. "That will be fine." Going to the stall with Amber and the colt, she let herself inside.

Eli admired her confidence and her caring. In fact he admired so many things about her.

"Does he nurse vigorously?" Hadley asked.

"Like there's no tomorrow," Eli responded with a grin.

"I should draw blood," Hadley said. "How do you feel about that?"

Eli knew if she did, lab results would tell him whether there was any infection or anemia. "That's fine," Eli agreed, knowing it had to be done.

"Temperature, heart and breathing rates are good," Hadley told him as she assessed Coco.

"They've bonded well."

"I can see that," Hadley said.

"He follows her no matter where she moves."

"What are you feeding her?" Hadley asked.

"Alfalfa hay. I've been keeping the stall cleaned out and dry. She lets me handle him," Eli said. "I've been rubbing him all over, touching his mouth and nose."

Hadley glanced at Eli. He held her gaze. He could feel that vibration between them, that attraction that had led to their kiss and the awkwardness afterward. No matter what she said, he had a feeling her visit today had more to do with that attraction between them than a thank-you for the pie or checking on Amber and the foal.

"Did you tell Brooks you were coming out here?" he asked.

"I did," she said. "I called him before I came. I didn't want him running out here unnecessarily. I like to finish what I start."

That was interesting. Did that mean she

wouldn't start something unless she could finish it? Another reason for her backing away from him. She'd be driving back to Bozeman soon.

Hadley didn't seem to mind his watching her. She worked quickly and competently, careful she didn't scare Amber or pose any threat. New moms could be protective even if they'd been calm during the whole pregnancy and before. Eli watched carefully, too, because he knew Hadley wasn't used to working with horses.

"You're becoming an expert with larger animals."

"I'm always looking to expand my résumé," she joked. Then she said, "Imagine flying into herds of wild animals, helping the horses that roam the ranges without proper care."

"You'd figure out how to give them care?"

"Sure would. Everything from vaccinations to helping them heal from injuries."

"Have you ever seen them in the wild?"

"I have…in the Big Horns. I went with some friends when I was in college. They were so majestic standing on the ridge above us as if they were greeting us. That was my first glimpse of them. How about you?"

"I spotted a herd in Colorado." He wasn't going to go into it. That was during his Elaine days. "I'm going to check and make sure everything's secure here, then we can go over to my cabin."

It took some effort for him to walk away from Hadley rather than going into that stall with her. But he didn't want to crowd Amber, and he didn't want to crowd Hadley. He imagined she could be even more skittish.

Fifteen minutes later Eli opened the door to his cabin, saying, "Home sweet home."

Hadley wasn't sure why she'd driven out here today. Sure, she'd told herself she wanted to thank Eli's mom and check on the horses. But deep in her heart, she knew her purpose had more to do with seeing Eli again. She was testing her reaction to him. Maybe she wouldn't feel that "zing" when he looked at her. Maybe she wouldn't remember their kiss in vivid detail. Maybe the attraction would have disappeared. Part of her hoped it had. The other part...

Eli had driven them from the barn in his truck, and Hadley had struggled to find conversation. Not because they didn't have things to talk about, but because Eli seemed to take up all her breathing space. Whenever she was around him, she felt breathless. She could try fooling herself, but there was no denying it. Their attraction was still there.

Now as he welcomed her into his home, she realized this was much more than just a cabin. Eli had said he'd decorated it himself with his sister's help, and it was well-done. Huge beams crisscrossed the ceiling with a loft at the far end and stairs leading to it. A stone fireplace was the center point of the room, and the rustic furniture with red Native American upholstery was mostly grouped about that. Bay windows surrounded the dining area, where there was a table large enough for four. Shiplap lined all the walls along with a wall hanging in cream, red and black. The same colors were featured in the rug on the wood floor.

"No flat-screen TV?" she asked, surprised.

He laughed. "I mostly stream on my laptop. I have a bigger monitor set up in the bedroom that I can always swivel toward the bed."

The mention of his bed had her seeing visions in her mind that had nothing to do with the holidays or sugarplums.

All of a sudden the kitten barreled down the steps, half jumping and half falling as it went. It came straight to Eli and rubbed on his jean-clad leg.

Hadley laughed out loud.

"I've named her," he said. "She's Winks, and her mom's name is Whisper because she travels more quietly and not as rambunctiously."

Eli was holding Winks now, and the kitten was rubbing her head against his coat.

The momma cat, Whisper, started down the stairs now, too, obviously checking on her offspring and following the voices. Hadley held her arms out for the kitten. "Can I have a look at her?"

"Sure," he said, shrugging out of his jacket. "The eyedrops are working."

Hadley unzipped her jacket and sat on the sofa with the kitten before her on the narrow, bench-like table where a coffee table book on the Southwest lay. Her focus was on the kitten as she examined her, but she couldn't help glancing around, too. Eli's floor-to-ceiling bookshelves near the dining area were filled. Just from looking at the spines, Hadley could tell he owned books on every subject imaginable.

"I would love to have a place like this someday," she said, meaning it.

"Where do you live now?" he asked, sitting on the sofa beside her. He wasn't too close, but close enough that she was aware of every inch of him from the thick hair on his head—he'd taken off his Stetson after they'd come in—to his jean-clad thighs and worn boots.

Her thoughts scrambled, and she had to re-assemble them to answer his question. "I rent the first floor of a house in town. I wanted somewhere convenient to the clinic."

"So if you take off someplace, you can leave it easily behind."

There was no censure in Eli's voice, yet she felt it was a little crisp, or maybe just the truth. "I suppose that's true. I never meant it to be permanent. I'm not there very much. What about you? Did you have a place before you built this?"

"I lived with my parents to save money and because we really are all a team. Then it was time I had a place of my own."

"How do you feel living apart from them? That had to be a change."

"It's a good change for all of us…and for Derek, too. I think when I was in the house he always felt I was looking over his shoulder. I never meant to give him that impression, but being an older brother and all that…"

"And your parents? How did they feel about your moving out?"

He gave her a questioning look as if he figured there was more behind her question than a simple answer. And maybe there was. When she'd been away at college, she'd known her parents had missed her, and they still hoped she wouldn't go that far away. But she wasn't sure where she wanted to settle. At least not anymore. She'd been willing to follow Justin Corrigan anywhere. Now she didn't think she'd give any woman the advice to do that.

Eli's voice brought her back from thoughts she'd rather forget. He said, "It's not like I'm in the next state. I'm still on the ranch, and I'm sure they're happy about that. Dad's getting older and he can't do what he once did, although he won't admit it. I can shoulder some of that for him. You know it's not something you put into words, but he knows I'm here when he needs me."

Yes, Eli was the dependable one. She shouldn't even put him in the same category with Justin. But after the fiasco with the veterinary pharmaceutical rep, she put all men in that category.

Whisper had insinuated herself between Eli's legs. Now she wound around Hadley's and then jumped up on the coffee table with her kitten. Hadley automatically checked her over, liking the care they both had been given.

Eli's voice was husky as he said, "I found an old wicker wash basket and filled it with a fleece blanket. That's up in my bedroom, and they seem to like that the best, at least for sleeping when I'm not here. When I'm home, they're down here with me."

"Have you ever had pets?"

"Not in the way you mean," he said with amusement in his voice. "There were always the horses and foals, and learning to get to know each one of them as they were born. Cats ran around the barn, and for a while Derek and I took care of a couple of goats. We were about ten. How about you?" he asked. "There had to be a reason why you became a vet."

"There was. I had a dog, the most adorable mutt that Dad had found along the road. He was my best friend for about five years. But then cancer took him. After it did, I decided the best thing I could learn to do was take care of animals. I find them homes when I can, so I haven't taken any home with me yet. My hours aren't conducive to having a pet, but I'd like to someday."

"The same way you'd like to have your own house?"

"You make it sound like a far-off dream."

"Isn't it?"

"Possibly. My sisters and my mom, and even my grandmother, seem to want me to make all my life decisions right now, and then be done with it. I don't feel that way. I'm still exploring each one as it comes along."

Eli thought about that. "Until you find exactly what you want."

As she gazed into his eyes, the sparkle there teased her into believing she wanted something entirely different from what they were talking about.

His voice was low when he said, "Hadley."

She knew what he wanted, and she knew what *she* wanted. Yet her past experience told her being attracted like this wasn't a good thing. She couldn't be impulsive. She couldn't be reckless. When she'd been both three years ago, her heart had been broken.

"Don't you feel it?" Eli asked, bringing her back to the moment.

"What?" Her voice was a mere whisper.

"The electricity."

"I'm leaving after Thanksgiving weekend," she reminded him.

"I know," he said solemnly. "But a kiss isn't a commitment."

She knew full well a kiss wasn't a commitment. She also knew that vows might not even be a commitment. So she did the only thing she could do. She stood and then she said in her most professional voice, "Whisper and Winks look good. You're doing a good job with them, Eli. I never expected you to—"

"Take cats into my house?" He was joking with her, but the joking didn't reach his eyes. She could tell he was thinking about what had almost happened on the sofa. So was she, but she couldn't dwell on it. She couldn't even entertain the thought of anything starting with Eli.

With her emotions in turmoil, she headed for his door.

He followed her, and they were outside on the way to the car when a snowball slammed Eli in the chest. He turned and spotted Derek grinning from ear to ear. Not only Derek, but four other good-looking men with him.

Shaking his head, Eli brushed the snow off his coat. "Hadley," he said, "these are some of my cousins—Garrett, Shawn, Booker and Cole. Along with another brother, Zach, they've been living here with my uncle Phil."

Hadley had heard the story about these Dalton brothers and their dad. A raging brush fire had burned down the family ranch, taking most of the animals and tragically, their mother. These Daltons, instead of splitting apart, had managed to stick together. They'd decided to come to Rush Creek Falls to start over.

Derek piped up, "Zach was staying here until he placed an ad in the *Rust Creek Falls Gazette* to seek a wife."

Garrett added, "He ended up falling in love with Lydia Grant, who'd worked at the *Rust Creek Falls Gazette*. They're living in a cottage on a ranch on the outskirts of town."

"I think my grandmother told me that they'll marry in the spring," Hadley said. News and gossip traveled quickly in Rust Creek Falls.

Eli's cousin Booker stooped down, scooped up snow and made another snowball. "So how about a real snowball fight, cuz?"

"Don't you boys have chores to do?" Eli asked with a mock scowl.

"All done," Shawn answered, making another snowball. "And I would imagine since Hadley here is a born-and-bred Montana girl, she'd go for a little snowball fight, too." He wiggled his brows at Hadley.

When had she last had some fun, real fun? And these young men seemed like they knew how to have it. She quickly put on the gloves that had been stuffed in her pocket, scooped up snow, made a missile out of it and tossed it at Booker. He tossed a snowball back, and it whacked her in the shoulder.

Eli said, "Hadley, if you don't want to do this—"

She made a nice rounded snowball and fired it at *him*. That must have done it for Eli because he entered into the fray. Soon snowballs were flying, and they were plowing through the snow after each other. In no time their coats were splattered with white and their cheeks had turned red.

Eli said to Hadley, "How long has it been since you've built a snowman?"

"You mean a snowwoman, don't you?"

Booker said, "Uh-oh. I'm out of here. Let *them* argue about women's rights."

The others mumbled and headed back toward the barn.

"They deserted," Hadley said after they'd gone.

Eli merely shrugged. Then he looked around at the snowbanks. "We could do this one of two ways. You could build a snowwoman and

I can build a snowman, or we can try to build a snow horse."

Hadley laughed at that compromise. "A snow horse it is."

For the next half hour that's what they did. And when they were finished, Hadley was rightly proud of it, too. They'd used an evergreen branch for the horse's tail, and Hadley had woven together some branches to wrap around its neck.

"How about some hot chocolate?" Eli asked Hadley. "It will warm you up before you have to drive home, and you can thank my mom in person for that pie."

She could have passed up the hot chocolate, but she really did want to thank his mother for the pie. So she agreed. "Warming up a bit would be nice."

Shaking the snow from their coats and boots, they piled into the truck and drove to the ranch house.

Hadley had a contented feeling she hadn't experienced for a very long time. Maybe it was from expending physical energy, or maybe it was because of enjoying sitting beside Eli in companionable silence. Hard to know.

Eli parked near the wide front porch. As soon as Hadley entered the Dalton house, she was encompassed by its feeling of warmth. It was because of the cozy furniture, the rugs on the plank flooring, the little touches that made a place a home. There was an aerial photograph of the ranch on one wall, along with knickknacks that Hadley imagined the children had given to their parents over the years.

As Eli escorted Hadley into the kitchen, she caught sight of Rita Dalton at the stove, stirring something in a huge soup pot.

"Hi there," Eli's mother said, her eyes lighting up. It was obvious she liked to have company.

"Hi, Mom. Remember Hadley? She was at Kayla's wedding."

"Of course I do. Melba talks about you all the time."

"Uh-oh," Hadley said. "My grandmother's as honest as they come. I'm not sure I want to know what she said."

"Come on, let me get you some hot chocolate and we can talk about it. Derek and his cousins ran through here a little while ago, but they didn't stay. You'll keep me company for a while, won't you?" she asked her son.

Eli raised his brows at Hadley, and she gave a little nod. He answered his mother, "Sure,

Mom," and took off his coat. Hadley did the same, and Eli hung both of them on pegs near the back door.

"You have a lovely house, Mrs. Dalton."

"I've been working at it for years. I should."

Hadley liked Eli's mother already.

Eli started for the cupboard and was about to pull down a box of hot chocolate mix, but his mother went over to him and said, "Not that stuff. I know you and Derek use it when you want something quick. I'm going to make the real thing. Get a saucepan for me."

"She melts chocolate into it and uses cream," Eli said to Hadley in a conspiratorial voice.

"I'm going to have to build another snow horse to burn off calories," Hadley decided.

"Nonsense," Rita protested. "You could use a few pounds, just like most women your age. Oatmeal raisin cookies to go with that hot chocolate?"

Hadley laughed again. "You make it hard to resist."

"The boys never do. Kayla and Kristen…" She wiggled her hand. "Sometimes they do. I'm making a pot of vegetable soup for supper tonight, but it will be fine on simmer. I imagine your sister Claire makes that, too."

Mostly everyone in town knew Claire worked at the boardinghouse and helped in the kitchen. She'd turned from a woman who hadn't cooked into a woman who cooked really well under their grandmother's tutelage. "This time of year is great for stews and soups and baked bread."

"I have a recipe for a cinnamon loaf Melba has been asking me to give her for years, but I keep telling her it's a family secret," Rita said with a wink.

Eli took the cookie tin over to the table and pointed to a chair for Hadley. He took the seat across from her. Rita turned from the saucepan at the stove and eyed the two of them with a smile.

Hadley could see that Eli gave his mother a shake of his head that was almost imperceptible. Still, Hadley caught it. Just what did that mean? That his mother shouldn't get any ideas about the two of them? That would certainly be best.

Nevertheless, as soon as the hot chocolate was made, Rita brought it to the table and poured it into three mugs. "I'll have some with you, but I'll forgo the whipped cream. I just happen to have some that I whipped up this morning. I was going to use it on apple cobbler tonight, but I can whip up more."

And before Hadley had any say in the matter, Rita had spooned two good tablespoons onto her hot chocolate. As it floated on the top, the scent of the chocolate and the warmth of it made Hadley feel…almost weepy. How could that be? Was she so unused to being around a man and being treated kindly that this was the result?

Apparently thinking the silence had gone too long, Rita said, "We'll soon be putting up a Christmas tree. How do you feel about Christmas, Hadley? Everybody has their own take on the holiday."

That was a thought-provoking question. She'd had reasons the past few years to work on the holiday. She still enjoyed choosing presents for loved ones, but the sparkle of Christmas just wasn't the same anymore. So she said, "I believe Christmas is for children."

"Oh, you do? Are you busy tomorrow?" Rita asked.

"Mom," Eli warned.

"Shush, boy," Rita said. "I'm talking to Hadley. And before you say whether you're busy or not, I'll tell you why I'm asking. We're having a big volunteer day at the community center tomorrow. We're filling food baskets for needy families. If parents feel they can provide for their children, they're more likely to make Christmas happier for their kids, don't you think?"

"I'm sure that's true," Hadley said. "Is there a toy drive, too?"

"Yes, there is, and not just store-bought toys. People actually make things for the children—crocheted stuffed animals, wooden trucks and trains, even old-fashioned games like painted checkerboards. No child in this town should be without a smile on Christmas morning."

"That's a wonderful idea, and I'd like to help. What time should I be there?"

Derek clapped Eli's shoulder as they passed the old-fashioned hitching post outside the Ace in the Hole later that night. "Ready for this viewing party?"

Eli's mind wasn't on viewing the latest episode of *The Great Roundup*, a cowboy/adventure reality show that his cousin Travis had signed up for. Brenna O'Reilly, another resident of Rust Creek Falls, was also participating. Rather, he was remembering each of his encounters with Hadley Strickland. The one that replayed in his mind the most was their kiss.

He glanced up at the wood-burned sign for the Ace in the Hole and the neon red sign with an ace of hearts playing card over the door. This bar could be a rough-and-rowdy cowboy hangout, depending on the clientele that particular night. There had been occasional rumbles and fights, but tonight couples would be attending to watch the latest episode of *The Great Roundup*. When he visited his cousin Trav during filming in July, Trav—Ben Dalton's son—and Brenna O'Reilly seemed to really be on the road to romance.

Eli opened the bar's old screen door with its rusty hinges and then the heavy wood door. Tonight no country tunes poured from the jukebox. Instead, the TV blared loud and clear. Booths lined the outer walls while wooden tables with ladder-back chairs formed a square around a small dance floor. A few cowboys played pool in the far back. As Eli glanced around, he briefly took in the framed Old West photos and those of local ranches that hung on the walls. Studying the wooden bar lining the right side of the room and its dozen bar stools, he spotted Hadley's cousins sitting there. He could see in the mirrored wall reflecting rows of glass bottles and customers at the bar that Hadley wasn't with them.

Eli spotted several couples he knew at the tables, among them his cousin Zach with his fiancée, Lydia. From two booths, Zach's brothers, Shawn, Garrett, Booker and Cole, waved Eli and Derek over.

They joined their cousins. Seated next to Booker, Eli opened his jacket but didn't shrug out of it. He wasn't sure how long he was going to stay.

When a waitress came rushing over, Eli ordered a beer while Derek, who'd sat across from him, requested scotch neat.

Booker elbowed Eli. "Did you ask the pretty vet for a date?"

Eli didn't particularly want his cousins poking into his private life. "Why are you asking?"

"Derek told me to."

Derek grinned at Eli. He couldn't possibly know what they were talking about because of the high volume level of the TV and the cheers that were rising from the crowd during the latest challenge on the show.

Eli just shook his head at both men and turned toward the TV. One of the challenges this week *was* cheer-worthy. He'd heard all about it during the preview that aired at the end of last week's episode. He watched as Brenna and his cousin Travis fought with all they were worth to win as the host timed them. It was easy for Eli to catch up with what was happening. The couple had to bring up a wooden box from the bottom of the pond. They dived over and over until together they hefted the box to the surface of the water. Swimming as fast as they could, they sputtered to shore and dragged the box to a spot where they could work on the locks. Apparently they'd earned keys before Eli had arrived. He could tell the couple's hands were shaking as they inserted a key in one of two padlocks and then focused on the other padlock.

Booker nudged Eli again. "*Are* you going to date Hadley? I've heard you haven't had a serious romance in years."

"*Serious* would be rough with Hadley living in Bozeman."

"So you've thought about it."

"I've thought about *her*," he admitted, then turned to the big-screen TV. "Now let's see if Trav can win this."

"He'll need Brenna's help," Booker said philosophically.

They watched as Brenna and Trav pulled a burlap bag from the box, untied the knots and then dumped the puzzle pieces onto a board provided for them. Eli decided that romantic relationships were just like that puzzle. All the pieces had to fit and make the perfect picture.

The Great Roundup had given him something to think about.

Saturday morning, Eli had been passing by the community center and decided to stop in. That was all there was to it, he told himself as he opened the door of the building and went inside. The center was bustling. He knew many of the people there, and they waved to him or said hello as he made his way through volunteers who were sorting food or boxing up items. One corner of the room was obviously dedicated to toy collection.

It didn't take him long to spot Hadley, not with that glossy, dark brown hair falling down her back, black leggings that disappeared into tall leather boots and a deep purple turtleneck sweater that dipped below her fanny. He noticed everything about this woman every time he was around her, though he still told himself he didn't want to.

His mother waved at him from a table across the room, and she pointed to Hadley and winked.

He knew he was playing right into his mom's hand. She wanted him to settle down so she had grandbabies. Or maybe she just wanted him to be happy.

Wasn't he happy? He had work he liked and family, a house of his own and now pets to share it. Still... His gaze returned to Hadley.

When he approached her, she smiled and then gave him a perplexed look. "What are you doing here?"

"I had errands. I had to stop at the feed store, so I thought I'd look in here and lend a hand if it was needed."

Lorna Babcock, a frizzy-haired sixty-year-old, called to him from the toy center. "Hey there, Eli. You here to help? We can use some strong arms to carry boxes."

"Wherever I can fit in."

"Just find yourself a spot. I'll call you when we need someone to haul."

"Do you need help?" he asked Hadley.

"Sure do. I need ten boxes pretty much filled evenly with everything I've got here, from the canned beans to the fruit cocktail. That would be great if you could carry them over to that corner that's going to be the distribution center. Someone there is labeling everything and tagging with names."

"I'm on it," Eli said. Taking off his jacket, he went to hang it on the portable coat hanger. When he returned, Hadley gave him a look that he did his best to ignore. He wasn't wearing anything different from any other day—a flannel shirt, jeans and boots. But when she looked at him, he felt she was assessing all of him. Did women do that?

She quickly looked away, her eyes darting to the canned goods in front of her. Because he didn't want to embarrass her or himself, he started a different type of conversation. "Sometimes I see Rust Creek Falls as an extension of ranch living. The town pulls together just like my family does."

"I heard about how all the residents helped each other after the flood. The town has made a remarkable recovery."

"Even the newcomers have made that happen," Eli said as he boxed a jar of peanut butter next to a bag of rice. He nodded to the table next to them. "That's Hudson Jones, who married Bella Stockton. Bella's a longtime resident. When Hudson and his brother Walker were newcomers, Hudson donated electronic tablets to the elementary school so the kids could learn better. There are a lot of Secret Santas that no one knows about."

"Secret Santas?" Hadley asked, looking for clarification.

Now he realized he messed up and he shouldn't have opened his mouth. But he had to explain. "Sure, people who give without anybody knowing they do it. The result is everybody's life is made better. It's just like these food baskets. They don't seem like much, but they could get a family through a couple of weeks. That's important in these times."

Hadley stopped sorting canned goods and gave him a curious look. She asked perceptively, "Are you a Secret Santa?"

"That word *secret* goes with Santa for a reason," he responded, not answering her one way or the other. But there was a warm look in her eyes, and he realized he couldn't fool her. But he wasn't going to say more either.

Suddenly Lorna was charging toward him and Hadley.

"Uh-oh," Eli said. "Lorna's on the move."

"Is that bad?"

"It means she's going to ask us to do something for her."

Marching right up to them, the older woman said, "I need a favor." She didn't wait for them to ask what, but went on, "Jazzy

Smith has asked for ten of the food baskets to give the residents she knows who would not want to be on an official list. But Brooks is tied up with a rancher outside Kalispell, and she's caring for his dad after surgery and can't pick them up. I need somebody to deliver them."

"I can deliver them," Hadley volunteered. "But I walked over here. I'll have to go get my SUV."

Before he caught his tongue, Eli said, "My truck is right outside. We can go together. I've never gotten a firsthand look at the Smith Rescue Ranch."

"It would be easier with two of you doing it," Lorna decided for them.

Hadley was looking unsure, as if his idea troubled her. However, she conjured up a smile. "We'll have ten of these ready in a few minutes," she told Lorna.

But Eli heard the uncertainty in her voice. Was this volunteer jaunt going to be awkward?

Chapter 7

On the drive to the Smith Rescue Ranch, it didn't take long for Eli to realize that Hadley looked and acted uncomfortable. He didn't have Derek's charm with the ladies. He only knew how to be honest. "You know," he said, "you should have vetoed the idea of us doing this together if you didn't want me to come along."

"I hated to refuse Lorna," she answered. "She thought she was doing a good thing."

That answer wasn't to his liking, but he didn't think Hadley was pushing him away just for the heck of it. There was something at the bottom of her reasoning.

"Are you a people pleaser?" he asked.

Out of the corner of his eye, he saw her study him. "Yes, I am."

"Care to tell me why?" For some reason, he didn't think people pleasing came naturally to Hadley; rather something had taught her to do it.

She was quiet for a few beats, but then she answered him. "I was bullied in elementary school. I was pudgy, short and an easy target. I was the last one picked for anybody's games. If I answered in class too often, I was made fun of. So I learned from that. I tried not to capture anybody's attention. I kept my mind on my schoolwork, increased my brainpower whenever I could, but didn't let others know about it. That paid off in high school because I earned a scholarship that helped with college."

Although he knew he should keep his eyes on the road, there wasn't any traffic and he gave her a long, appraising male look. "You're too pretty to fly under the radar now."

Her gaze met his for a second before he turned his attention back to the road. "That's not a line," he assured her. For once she didn't say anything, though he didn't know if she believed him. Whether he should prod or not, he did. "Did the bullying affect your adult life?"

"I might want to please the people I care about and those who care about me. But overall, the bullying made me bolder as an adult. I push the limits now more and I stand up for what I believe in. In fact, now sometimes I'm too impulsive."

"Like when you kissed me back?"

She didn't hesitate to say, "Exactly like that."

They rode in quiet for the next mile, but then she asked him, "How did your childhood affect *your* adult life?"

He gave a shrug. "I told you, being the oldest made me feel responsible for everybody. I felt my parents depended on me to be the practical, steady one."

"Don't you get tired of that? Don't you ever want to break out and just have fun?"

"I find ways to do that now and then."

"The Daltons do have a reputation with women."

He gave her a sharp look. Then he realized that was probably true. Derek certainly did. Jonah was married now, but he'd done his fair share of dating. Eli had to admit he had, too. Only, after Elaine he hadn't been serious about it.

He glanced over at Hadley. He knew her well

enough to know she didn't want to be anybody's conquest. And, from her body language, he also realized the subject was closed...for now.

Hadley felt bad about the silence between her and Eli on the rest of the drive to the ranch. But she hadn't known what else to say. The Daltons were all sexy men who could date whomever they wanted to date. And Derek and Eli, according to the gossip, hadn't seemed serious about anybody they'd dated. Not recently anyway. That told Hadley they were out for a good time.

Yet Eli didn't seem like a carefree Romeo. Still, after the hard work he did, maybe on the weekend he just wanted an outlet like many men did. It was impossible to know.

As she and Eli walked up to the front door of Jazzy and Brooks's home, she wished she could relax around Eli more. She wished—

No, she didn't. She'd stopped wishing. She knew better than to dream about hearts and flowers, and a romance that could last forever.

She reached the door first and knocked. When Jazzy answered, she looked frazzled. Her hair was mussed, and she appeared tired.

After Hadley and Eli had stepped inside, she asked Jazzy, "Are you okay?"

Jazzy gave her a weak smile. "I've got to admit taking care of one recalcitrant patient is harder than caring for a whole stable of horses. Brooks's dad thinks he should be better already." She shook her head and then looked at Eli. "Maybe you could talk some sense into Barrett, man-to-man, because he's not listening to me. I think he might already be regretting the decision to move in here with me and Brooks. Brooks has tried to talk to him, but father-and-son communication…" Jazzy shook her head again. "Sometimes that just doesn't work so well. Barrett thinks Brooks is being condescending, and Brooks thinks Barrett is just being stubborn."

Hadley saw how worried Jazzy was about it, so she sought to reassure her. "This might not be about you and Brooks at all. It could just be that Barrett's worried about losing his independence."

Eli immediately agreed. "Men like my dad and Brooks's dad—they need to think they control at least their own world if not everybody else's. Didn't Barrett try to arrange your marriage to Brooks?"

Now Jazzy laughed. "He was a huge part of why we married. But I've got to admit, Brooks and I do belong together."

"Then maybe what you need to do," Eli suggested, "is to make Barrett feel he's more in control."

"And how do I do that?" Jazzy asked.

"I'm not sure," Eli told her. "But I'll think about it while I'm unloading the baskets. Where do you want me to put them?"

Jazzy pointed to a corner of the living room. "Over there would be good for now. We'll be delivering them soon. While you do that, I'll make coffee. Hadley, do you want to help?"

Hadley didn't know what kind of help she'd be making coffee, but it was obvious Jazzy wanted to talk to her. So she followed her into the kitchen.

Jazzy took out a coffee canister. "Grab the milk from the refrigerator, would you?" she asked Hadley as she dumped the water into the coffeemaker. "So tell me, how do you like Eli?"

Hadley unzipped her jacket and groaned. "Not you, too."

"What do you mean, not me, too?"

"My sisters asked all kinds of questions, and Claire and Tessa aren't easy to stonewall. My grandmother wasn't too subtle either."

Jazzy eyed her before she took a small pitcher from the cupboard and poured milk into it. "From what I've heard, Eli is a good guy, loyal to his family and friends. You certainly would want that quality in a guy you dated, wouldn't you?"

Hadley gave it serious thought because this was Jazzy who was asking, and they'd become friends. "I would want that quality in a guy, but I'd want an adventurous spirit, too. I'm not sure Eli has that." She didn't mean to be that blunt, but she knew Jazzy would push as much as Claire or Tessa if she didn't give her honest answers.

After Jazzy set the milk pitcher on the table, she asked Hadley, "Do you know that Eli used to be a rock climber?"

Hadley's eyes widened in surprise.

"And he took trips to the Mexican ruins and the Alaskan glaciers. But that was when—" Jazzy stopped. She might have even stopped on purpose to force Hadley to ask questions.

All right, well, now Hadley did have some questions. "Go on," she encouraged her friend. "What were you going to say?"

Jazzy shrugged. "I go out with friends now and then. I don't just see horses and Brooks."

Hadley gave her an understanding smile.

"When we go to the Ace in the Hole, I hear talk…from the girls and from the people they know. The talk always seems to turn to the guys."

"So what did you hear about Eli?"

"Out of high school, he dated Elaine Nixon. She worked for a local insurance office. They were serious, and she had an adventurous spirit, and it seemed he did, too, back then. Together they'd find the best travel deals at slow times at the ranch. They dated for two years. They took a few jaunts to Mexico, and as I said, they visited the Alaskan glaciers, too, by helicopter. She'd go with Eli when he went rock climbing, and he taught her a lot about it. But then Elaine left town to take a job in Chicago because she was tired of small-town life. Rumor has it, she wanted Eli to go with her. But that wasn't what he wanted. Apparently after she left, his adventurous spirit just seemed to fade away."

Hadley heard noise coming from the living room and realized it was Eli bringing in the baskets. Her conversation with Jazzy ended, giving her a lot to think about as she took mugs from a mug tree and lined them up on the counter.

Eli knocked on the door of Barrett Smith's suite and heard a gruff, "Come in."

When he opened the door, he saw Barrett in a recliner, his leg propped up on a pillow. He was a barrel-chested man with gray hair and ruddy cheeks. Eli knew he was about six feet tall, but in the recliner he looked shorter and older.

As soon as Brooks's dad saw Eli, however, he grinned and sat up a little straighter. "Good to see you, boy. What are you doing here?"

"I came over with Hadley Strickland to drop off some baskets from the community center. Jazzy's going to distribute them to people who don't want their name on an official list."

"I get that. Some folks want to keep their pride. How's your dad?"

"He's good."

"I heard Hadley tended to your mare. I wish I could have done that for you. I've tended to Dalton horses for years."

Eli had known Barrett Smith since he was a boy. "I figured you probably miss what you like to do. That's why I stopped in to tell you Amber and her foal are doing really well. Hadley was great. She helped with the breech birth."

"She did, did she? She's like Brooks, up-and-coming vets when I'm on my way out."

"Do you *want* to retire?" Eli asked.

Barrett pointed to his knee encased in loose sweatpants. "I don't know as if I have a choice. If I had my druthers, I'd still be working part-time. We'll see what happens. I might sell my place and my practice and just help out Brooks when he needs it. I'll tell you one thing. I don't like feeling like an invalid."

"I know you don't. Nobody does. But you *are* one, at least for a short while. It hasn't been that long since your surgery."

Barrett frowned and looked down at the knee again. "I suppose you're right. That's what Jazzy and Brooks keep telling me. But I feel like I should be doing more. I hate just sitting here watching TV."

"You know, don't you, the more you fight it, the longer it's going to take to get better? Why don't you just let Jazzy pamper you? It isn't just for your benefit. That will make her feel like she's helping you."

Barrett looked like he was going to seriously consider Eli's words. He pointed to the armchair beside his recliner. "Sit down for a few minutes. Talk to me about what matters—ranching, animals, your family. I hear you have a houseful."

Eli spent the next fifteen minutes or so

keeping Barrett company. The older man seemed starved for some talk and opinions about what was happening in Rust Creek Falls.

When Eli left Barrett with the promise to visit again soon, he returned to the living room, where Hadley and Jazzy were talking. They stopped when he came in, making Eli suspicious. Were they talking about him?

He motioned to Barrett's suite. "I had a few ideas while I was in there with him that could help all of you."

Jazzy was altogether interested. "Tell me."

"First of all, get one of those portable intercom systems, or a walkie-talkie. Let him call you when he needs you instead of your checking on him so often. That way he wouldn't feel like such a burden."

Jazzy was already nodding. "That's a great idea. I don't know why we didn't think of it."

"Because you're in the middle of the situation," he said. "I also noticed that once he started talking, he didn't want to stop. I think he's starved for a little companionship. You've got to remember, he was treating clients all day, as many as he could fit in. So he had lots of people interaction as well as pet action."

"And what can I do about that?" Jazzy asked, worried.

"Invite a couple of his friends in to play checkers or cards."

Listening up to now, Hadley chimed in, "I bet Old Gene would enjoy a visit and a game with him. In fact, he might like a break from everybody at the boardinghouse. It sure is noisy there. And my grandmother doesn't need his help with so many people around."

"Those are both great suggestions," Jazzy said. "It's serendipitous that you two dropped off the baskets." She gave her attention to Eli. "You've never taken a tour of the barns and the horses. If you want to, now's a great time. My part-time helper, Darby Conrad, is out there now. She can answer any of your questions. So can Hadley, for that matter. She's been here often enough to know most of the horses and our routine."

Eli glanced at Hadley. "Do you have time?"

"I'm not on the clock. Sure, I have time."

The path to Jazzy and Brooks's barn still had a layer of snow. Hadley's boots made impressions as they walked, but that wasn't what held her rapt attention. It was the cowboy next to her. She cast a covert glance at Eli. After her conversation with Jazzy, she had trouble seeing him in a different light. He was a rock climber? He'd explored Mexican ruins and Alaskan glaciers? He hadn't mentioned traveling during their snowbound time together. Yesterday, he had mentioned the wild horses he'd seen in Colorado. With Elaine?

He wasn't one of those silent-cowboy types. Yet she had the feeling that he was a very private person. Certainly she respected that. She'd become private about her personal life. And just like her, she was sure there was a reason he was quiet about his, too.

"There are two barns," she explained, giving him another considering look.

"I can see the one has long pens attached that separate the horses," he noted. "That's essential for wild mustangs, and I guess it would be good for horses who have been abused, too."

"Until they learn to trust," Hadley agreed.

When they walked into the larger of the two barns, Eli said, "I can tell this is a new barn. The smells are different than in a decades-old one."

"Tradition means a lot to you, doesn't it?"

"It does. I learned from my dad before I could talk, I imagine the same way he learned from his. Handing down a legacy is important, and caring for the land and the animals the best way possible. Family customs matter, too."

The door to the barn was propped open, and they walked along the stalls. Eli seemed to gravitate toward a stall with the nameplate Gypsy.

"Jazzy told me about Gypsy the last time I was here," Hadley explained. "She's a fairly new rescue who was left to starve when the owners moved away and abandoned her. She's sweet and wants to trust, but she's afraid."

He looked at her. "I thought you didn't relate to horses so well."

"Not that I don't relate. I just haven't cared for them the way I've cared for small pets. I feel more confident with other animals because I've had more experience with them. But I like horses."

He must have accepted her response because he didn't challenge it. Instead, he had his eyes on Gypsy. He didn't approach the horse, or even reach out his hand. He just stood there quietly appreciating the Appaloosa, then he started a conversation with the horse. "You know, don't you, that everybody here wants to take care of you. They won't abandon you. They'll feed you and water you and groom you. Soon you'll remember what it's like to run across a field and enjoy it, or to carry a human on your back who wants to know you, not use you."

Hadley watched, amazed, as Gypsy turned her head toward Eli, then she lifted it and her eyes seemed to study him.

"You were meant to have a good life," he told her, and she took a step toward him.

He waited a beat, then he slowly lifted his hand and held it out to her. She sniffed at his fingers. He let her, not attempting to do more than just get to know her. Finally, she nosed his palm. He ran his hand up her neck and under her mane.

Jazzy had been making progress with Gypsy and so had Brooks. But the mare was still skittish around them. With Eli, however, she'd already seemed to have given her trust. He'd made a connection so quickly. Hadley was impressed again with his gentleness and his horse-whisperer tendencies.

She stayed where she was so as not to disturb their communication, but she asked, "How did you learn to communicate with horses?"

"There's nothing magical about it," he said

in the same low voice he'd used to talk to Gypsy. "Once upon a time there was a Native American who lived in a hut not far from our property's boundary line. He lived meagerly with the bare essentials. But that's all he wanted. I used to sit and listen to his stories. He knew everything there was to know about horses. I followed him around and split wood for him. In exchange, Joe made me fried bread. He spent some time with our horses, too. He died when I was in high school, but I'll never forget what he taught me."

"What was that?"

"That nothing's more important than patience, observation, a gentle voice and a kind hand."

"He sounds like a wise man."

"He was."

Hadley would have liked to have found out more, but just then the barn door opened and Darby Conrad barreled in. She was blonde and tall and had enough energy for two Energizer Bunnies. She was young, in her early twenties, and when she spotted Eli, Hadley saw her flip her hair and widen her eyes. She was in flirt mode, that was obvious.

She walked straight up to Eli and extended

her hand. "Hi there. I'm Darby Conrad. Who are you?"

Eli's lips twitched with amusement, and Hadley thought he gave Darby one of those male appraising looks. "Eli Dalton is the name. I'm a friend of Brooks's. I understand you work here part-time."

"I do. I wish I could give it more hours, but I help my mom in her hair salon." She held up her hands, and her nails were painted bright pink. "I know it seems a little odd to have a manicure when you work in a barn, but it helps keep my nails in shape." She sauntered a little closer to Eli. "I suppose you love horses, too? Everybody around here does. I have a quarter horse named Moses. I barrel race with him."

"Do you participate in any rodeos?" Eli asked, as if he were interested.

At that, Hadley felt left out, so she wandered away. She went down the line until one of Jazzy's favorite horses, Clementine, a beautiful Chestnut, stuck her head over the stall in Hadley's path.

Hadley stepped up to the horse and rubbed her neck. She suddenly felt as if she were back in high school, and one of the popular cheerleaders had sneaked into the conversation that she was having with one of the boys in her class. One of the boys whom she wished would think of her as more than just a classmate. It was silly, really, that Darby could make her feel that way. But her time with Justin and the consequences of it had done a number on her self-esteem. At least in the way she related to men. She was overly careful now and much too guarded. She understood that, but she didn't know how to get beyond what had happened. Most of all, she didn't know how to trust again because of Justin's lies.

She didn't know how long she stood there thinking about it, everything that had happened, and why she couldn't seem to get beyond the past to find a future. She heard the back barn door open and shut, but she stayed where she was.

Soon Eli came up beside her. "Why did you wander away?"

"I didn't want to intrude." As soon as she said the words, she wondered if that was the truth. Or was the problem deeper than that? No, she couldn't have been jealous!

"You wouldn't have intruded," Eli insisted. "Nothing was going on. We were just talking about her latest rodeo."

"You're blind if you don't think anything was going on. Darby was flirting and you were flirting back."

"I was just having a conversation," he protested.

Deciding to take the bull by the horns, so to speak, Hadley focused on him instead of the horse. "Can you be honest with me about something?"

"Sure, I can be." He sounded certain.

"Were you attracted to Darby?"

He mulled over the question for an instant, but then he shrugged. "Not nearly as much as I'm attracted to *you*."

That comment made her speechless, and she didn't know what to say to it. But she had to come up with something, and she had to come up with it fast. So she fell back on the first thing that floated into her mind. "We'd better get back to town before Lorna sends out a search party."

"You could call her and tell them you're going to be delayed," he suggested, still with that calm, cool manner he had that frustrated her.

"And why am I going to be delayed?"

"I'd like to make a stop at my brother Jonah's office. I thought you might like to go with me. His architect office is a refurbished

Victorian. It's quite impressive. I thought you might like to see it."

"And you need to see him right now?"

"He just got back from a business trip. I know Mom would like him and his wife, Vanessa, to come to dinner, and I thought with a face-to-face meeting I might be able to convince him better than in a text or over the phone."

"He doesn't see your parents much?"

"Ever since Uncle Phil and his boys moved in with us, Jonah has kept out of the commotion. I can't blame him. There are usually lots of conversations going on and not enough time to talk to any one person. Do you know what I mean?"

"Sure do. It's like that at the boardinghouse right now." She thought about seeing Jonah's office, and then she said, "I really do like Victorians. The boardinghouse has lots of nooks and crannies."

"Melba's place is a gem…not only for its architecture but for the news that's generated there."

"For sure. I can't help but hear gossip. I can't be around my grandmother or my sisters without getting an earful."

Actually, Tessa, Claire and her grandmother wanted to pull her into the drama and romance in Rust Creek Falls, and there had been a lot of it. But Hadley kept herself removed as much as she could. It wasn't easy. And truth be told, she *was* interested in everything that happened here. How could she stay removed from lovers who had found each other? Claire and Levi had renewed their marriage, and Tessa had found true love with Carson.

She was still thinking about that a half hour later as Eli drew up in front of a beautiful Victorian house. She hopped out of the vehicle before he could come around and open her door. But there was a giant snowbank to climb over to get to the sidewalk. Eli saw that. His long legs easily topped it. Once he was on the sidewalk, he offered her his hand. "I can help you climb over, or I can lift you over."

The idea of being lifted in Eli's arms actually made her giddy. That's exactly why she said, "I'll take a hand in climbing over." Still, that didn't work out exactly as she'd planned.

Eli took both of her hands. As she gazed into his eyes, the brim of his Stetson shaded his face. Somehow her booted foot sank into the snow mound. She would have lost her balance and fallen, but Eli's large hands caught her around the waist.

"Easy," he said, his voice deep and husky.

Easy. It would be so easy to fall into her attraction for him. She concentrated on extricating her foot from the snowdrift, but as she did, she leaned forward and practically slid down the other side. Eli caught her, his arms going around her, holding her tight against him. She lost any desire to breathe. When she looked up at him, she knew what he wanted, and she wanted it, too. He was warmth and all man, and his sizzling sexuality just seemed to encompass her. *Remember Justin*, a warning voice in her head yelled at her.

Oh, she remembered Justin.

And Eli must have seen the ghost of that memory on her face because he leaned away. "What's wrong?"

Clamoring for the first viable excuse, she glanced around. "We're on a public sidewalk. You know Rust Creek Falls. Everyone will talk." She pulled out of his embrace and righted herself in her boots, standing firmly on solid ground once more.

"They'll only talk if there's something to talk about. Is there, Hadley?" Eli stood there, tall, handsome and questioning as he waited for her answer.

Chapter 8

For a few moments, Eli thought Hadley was going to be honest with him and tell him there was something between them that other people would notice and maybe even talk about. But he saw the exact moment when she decided that wouldn't be a good idea…that being too vulnerable around him wasn't even a possibility.

Taking a step back, she acted as if he hadn't even asked the question. "This is attractive," she said, turning toward Jonah's office. She took a few paces toward the steps. "Coming?" she asked.

He gave her a long, steady glare. "You didn't answer my question."

This time instead of evading him, she responded, "I don't think that's a conversation to have in the cold on a public sidewalk."

"Meaning we'll have that conversation sometime in a warmer spot?"

"We'll see," she said, and he knew she meant it.

Apparently she still hadn't made up her mind about him, though what there was to decide he didn't know. He suspected Hadley Strickland didn't give her trust easily, and he wanted to know the reason why. She'd been right. That definitely *wasn't* a conversation for a public sidewalk.

He led the way up the steps to the porch, and she followed him. After he opened the doors into the foyer, he immediately spotted his brother sitting at a desk to the left in his office.

From the doorway, Eli asked him, "Are you busy?"

"Not too busy for you," Jonah said, standing. "This is a surprise."

"Jonah, I don't know if you know Hadley Strickland."

Hadley stepped up to shake Jonah's hand and studied Eli's brother, who was six feet tall with dark hazel eyes. As usual, he was wearing a dress shirt and jeans with his boots.

"I think we've met in passing," Hadley said. "I've admired your wife's mural at the resort more than once."

Eli wasn't surprised. Everyone in Rust Creek Falls knew of the mural that depicted the history of the town. Vanessa's painting graced the lobby of the restored Maverick Manor.

"I'll tell Vanessa you've admired it," Jonah said. He addressed his brother again. "And how are you enjoying living in your new house? Are you finally settled in?" He looked at Hadley. "This guy bought his furniture piece by piece. It took a while for him to get it furnished."

"I wanted to be comfortable," Eli protested. "And I am."

"It's a beautiful house," Hadley said.

"You've seen it?" Jonah asked with a raised brow.

"Hadley's a vet," Eli explained. "Amber had her foal and a little trouble. We also found a cat and a kitten, so I took them in and she came in to check on them."

"You have pets?" Jonah rolled his eyes then shook his head. "I shouldn't be surprised.

There wasn't any doubt you'd put down roots here."

"And now you have, too," Eli pointed out. Jonah had spent years in Denver, till he met Vanessa.

"Yes, I have."

"I couldn't imagine living anywhere else," Eli confided, but then he remembered how his desire to stay here to ranch, to appreciate the land, had separated him from the woman he thought he'd loved.

"Now that I'm back, I can't imagine it either," Jonah agreed.

"Even though Vanessa and I haven't been to dinner lately, I do talk to Mom, you know. She said you'd be helping the Bonners with some repairs."

"That's in my plans for tomorrow," Eli said.

"You do good work, Eli. Lots of elderly folks are glad you're around."

At that Hadley gave him a questioning look, but he didn't explain.

"Speaking of Mom… She wanted me to ask you and Vanessa to come to dinner. I figured you couldn't shut me down face-to-face."

Jonah motioned to his desk. He had blue-prints and papers stacked there. "I'm not avoiding the family," he said. "I'm just busy. Vanessa has been, too. She was awarded a commission to paint a mural in a hotel in Denver. She just got back."

"Can you come over Monday night for dinner? Uncle Phil and his sons are going into Kalispell. It would just be me and Derek and the folks."

"I'll check with Vanessa. That sounds like a good idea. We'll be there for Thanksgiving, but I'm sure it will be bedlam."

"Do you want to give Mom a call after you check with Vanessa about Monday night?"

"Sounds good," Jonah said. He smiled at Hadley. "It was nice seeing you again."

A few minutes later they were back in the truck. Hadley fastened her seat belt and asked Eli, "So you're helping the Bonners?"

"Do you know them?"

"My grandmother does. When I'm here and we go to church, she usually manages to talk to all her neighbors. If I remember correctly, Mrs. Bonner had a stroke about six months ago."

"That's right. She's recovering, but her husband worries about her."

"Grandmother told me that they couldn't afford to have many renovations done."

"That's why I'm helping them," he admitted.

"And Jonah said you do good work, which means you've helped others. So you *are* a Secret Santa, too." There was a twinkle in her eye and amusement in her voice.

"You could call me that if you want, but I just help people who need it. There are lots of older folk who can't afford someone to do the work and don't have kids who can do it for them."

"Tell me why you do it."

He shrugged and started up the truck. "I'm not the most educated man in the world, but I've got skills. It's good karma to share them." He wouldn't have told Hadley about the work he did. That just wasn't his way. But now that she knew—

"So if you know the Bonners, would you like to come along with me tomorrow? If you've got something else on your schedule, I understand."

"Nothing on my schedule. Not unless I get another emergency call from Brooks. If I come with you, is there something I can do to help?"

"Can you cook?"

"I wouldn't be my grandmother's granddaughter if I didn't know how to cook."

"Maybe you could bring fixings along to make a meal. I'll tell the Bonners we'll provide dinner. That would be a treat for them. They don't get that many visitors, so I'm sure they'll enjoy our company, too."

"I like that idea. I like it a lot. Thanks for inviting me along, Eli."

"Maybe I have an ulterior motive," he replied as he pulled away from the curb. "Maybe when we're not on a public sidewalk, and we're someplace warm," he added as he cast a heated glance her way, "we can have that conversation you avoided."

The next day as Carl Bonner invited Hadley and Eli inside the small home, Hadley remembered what Eli had said yesterday. He couldn't imagine living anywhere but Rust Creek Falls. He was a man with roots. Did he stay because of the ranch and his family's land? Did he stay because he liked Rust Creek Falls? Did he stay because the small town was familiar, or maybe it was simpler than all that—he stayed because his family and friends were here.

Hadley thought about her own life in Bozeman. Tessa and Claire no longer lived there. She alternated her life with her husband from

California to Falls Mountain. Hadley's parents were in Bozeman, but their lives were busy and hers was, too.

Eli was carrying grocery bags, and so was Hadley. Seeing that, Carl said, "It looks as if you brought enough supplies for a week's worth of meals. I don't need no charity." The man was easily in his seventies with a white mustache and a balding pate that sported a few white strands.

"It's not charity," Hadley assured him. "I just thought after Eli does a little work, we can all use a home-cooked meal. I'm going to make a beef, noodle and tomato casserole. How does that sound?"

"That sounds just fine," Carl said with an answering smile. "I thought you were going to do something fancy with all those bags."

Suddenly Jill Bonner appeared in the doorway from the kitchen. She was using a four-pronged cane and didn't look the steadiest on her feet. Her husband went to her and helped her to an armchair in the living room.

"Do you remember Hadley Strickland from church?" he asked his wife.

"Oh, of course I do. Melba talks about you all the time," Jill told Hadley. She had snowy-white hair that looked like a halo around her head. She was thin, and her cardigan sweater looked oversize on her small frame. She was wearing sweatpants and a top that looked easy to pull on and off.

Hadley went to her and crouched down beside her chair. "Before I start supper, how would you like a cup of tea?"

"You don't have to go to any bother. Carl makes fine tea."

"I'm sure he does, but he's probably going to want to supervise Eli, don't you think?"

Jill gave a little giggle and said in a low voice, "You know how men operate, don't you?"

All too well, Hadley thought. "Let's just say my dad and grandpa would do the same." She leaned toward Jill conspiratorially. "Do you think hc'd like some apple cobbler for dessert tonight?"

"That sounds grand," Jill assured her. "Is yours as good as Melba's?"

"I doubt it," Hadley said with a laugh. "But I'll make a good attempt, and I'll put together a salad so no one can say we didn't have our vegetables."

"The tea kettle's on the stove," Jill explained. "And the mugs are on the counter. We don't bother putting them away."

"I'm sure I'll find everything without a problem."

Eli said, "I'll just put these groceries in the kitchen then go get my tools and we'll get started."

The next few hours sped by. Hadley made tea for her and Jill, then started supper. Afterward, she and Jill talked. They had a lot to talk about—from her grandmother and grandfather to events at church to Hadley's practice in Bozeman. Jill even showed Hadley how she managed to crochet, telling her it was good therapy for her hand that was still a little weak from the stroke. She made mistakes but she could correct them.

Hadley wished all of life was like that. Correctable.

After they all sat down to dinner, Hadley learned that the Bonners had a son who was living in Portland.

"We wish he'd move back here," Jill said honestly. "Not so he can take care of us, but just so we can keep company with him in the time we have left. I'm sure your parents feel the same," she said to Hadley.

Hadley didn't know. She'd rarely talked to her parents about anything like that. But she bet Eli had spoken with his parents about it.

His family bonds were one of the reasons he was so grounded and knew where he belonged.

Hadley had made sure she cooked enough food that the Bonners would have leftovers. After dinner, Eli helped her clean up while Carl showed Jill the improvements Eli had made to the bathroom.

While Eli plucked a dish from the drainer, ready to dry it, he told Hadley, "Carl's pleased with the repairs. I'm going to come back next week and build a ramp for the back steps. And you did a great job with supper. They should have enough for a couple of meals. Did you see Jill's face when she ate that real whipped cream on top of the apple cobbler? We made them happy, Hadley."

"It was easy to do. I can see why you enjoy helping. Maybe *enjoy* isn't the right word, but you find satisfaction in it."

"I usually enjoy it, too. Purpose is everything."

"Purpose?" she asked.

"Sure. Your purpose is getting up each day and helping as many animals as you can, right?"

"I suppose it is," she said thoughtfully. But then she wondered if that was enough of a purpose for her life.

She was still thinking about that as Eli drove her back to the boardinghouse. After he pulled up in front, he cracked a window and let the heater run along with the engine. "Are you ready to have that conversation now?"

She knew exactly what conversation he meant. But, no, she wasn't ready to have it. Still, she knew she couldn't avoid it.

"Eli, what do you want me to say?"

"This has nothing to do with what I *want* you to say. I want to know how you *feel*. There's chemistry between us, maybe even something more than that. But if it's all one-sided, you can hop out of this truck and I won't call you or expect you to visit Amber and Coco or the cats ever again."

When she thought about not seeing Eli again, she had a sick feeling in her stomach. Worse than that, her heart hurt a little. Oh, no. Her heart couldn't be involved.

"Eli, I'm not going to be here much past Thanksgiving."

He shrugged. "It's not like Bozeman is that far away."

No, it wasn't, she supposed. But long distance was no way to start a relationship. What was she even thinking? She didn't *want* a relationship.

Eli turned fully toward her and gently clasped her shoulder. As he nudged her toward him, he said, "I enjoy your company, Hadley."

She swallowed hard. "And I enjoy yours. This afternoon was pleasant." Better to stay on safe territory.

Even in the dim light from the dashboard she could see his small smile. "I was thinking more about the intimate time we shared in the barn."

"We didn't have any intimate time. We both had our clothes on," she pointed out.

"Do you think clothes make a difference?" he joked.

"I know clothes make *all* the difference in the world."

He suddenly grew serious. "I suppose that's true. If we'd taken off our clothes, we would have really found out what intimacy was."

"Eli," she warned.

"Does the idea of being intimate with me make you want to back away?"

Actually the exact opposite was true, but she couldn't admit that.

"Why are you so afraid to give in to this attraction?"

"Maybe attraction has gotten me into trouble before," she blurted out.

Although she suspected he might drop the subject, he didn't. "Do you want to tell me about it?"

"No, I don't. I just mean attraction is limited and sometimes doesn't go anywhere."

"But it could be a lot of fun finding out exactly where it's going to go," Eli protested.

Eli always seemed to carry the scent of leather and soap about him. It drew her to him, almost as much as anything else about him. Though she did like his eyes and his heavy brows and the jut of his jaw and the set of his lips. She was crazy for even thinking about becoming more involved with him. Not that she *was* involved. She could put the brakes on at any time. She could leave Rust Creek Falls and forget all about him.

But right now, sitting in his truck, so close to him, inhaling that soap and leather, inhaling him, watching his expression, feeling the electricity that ricocheted between them when they were in a confined space, she couldn't deny she was very attracted to him. If she could just take a moment to think… However, she didn't. She acted on impulse.

She reached up to his face and ran her thumb over the dent in his chin. IIe clasped her hand and did something she totally didn't expect. He kissed her fingers, one by one. Then he slid his hand under her hair at her neck, pulled her close and kissed her.

There was no doubt she was kissing him back this time. There was no doubt they were both involved in this kiss up to their eyeballs and down to their boots. Eli seemed to have the expertise and the power to make her feel more like a woman than she'd felt in years. She felt sensations deep inside that pushed her closer to him. Her fingers ached to touch him. They tunneled into his hair, knocking his hat off.

He didn't seem to mind because he kissed her harder, longer and wetter. The windows steamed up, and she decided breathing was overrated.

Suddenly the porch light went on and blazed through the car windows. They both became aware of it, blinked and slowly ended the kiss. Hadley felt embarrassed that she'd gone from zero to ten on the passion scale in a matter of seconds.

She mumbled, "I wonder if that thing's on a timer, or Old Gene is turning it on intentionally."

Eli's voice was husky when he said, "It could be Melba. She'll want you to know you have backup if you need it."

Hadley could have used backup three years ago…backup against her own foolishness. Backup to sit her down and explain what the wise thing to do would be. But she'd been besotted with Justin, and wisdom might not have entered into it either.

Before she could pull completely away, Eli stroked her cheek. "Hadley, there's nothing wrong with what we did."

"I know that. I'm still not sure it's wise."

Even though Hadley said it, she was reluctant to get out of the truck. Eli didn't seem eager to move away either. She racked her brain for something to say, something to bridge the silence. "So you'll be having a big Thanksgiving dinner on Thursday?"

"We will. It hasn't been decided yet where the celebration will take place—at the Circle D or at the Dalton family ranch, Uncle Ben's place. But it will be big and noisy with more food than even the Dalton clan can eat. They'll all be there, except for Kayla. She'll be spending Thanksgiving with you Stricklands. I suppose your celebration will be huge, too."

She nodded. "Melba and Old Gene will be in their glory having everybody. It will be noisy with lots of food and lots of teasing."

"You don't like the teasing part?"

Apparently Eli was beginning to know her, the nuances in her voice. She supposed her expression gave her away, too. "Maybe I'm just not a crowd person. Give me a litter of puppies and I'm fine. But give me a crowd of people, and I'd rather be holed up with one person, talking."

"I can relate to that," he said, with a smile in his voice. "Especially if that one person is the pretty lady in the truck with me."

He leaned over to give her another kiss, but she braced her hands on his chest. "I think I'd better go in." She unfastened her seat belt and moved over to the door.

"If I don't see you before you leave, Hadley, well—" He paused a moment before he added, "I have your phone number and you have mine."

She had it. But when she went back to Bozeman, she wouldn't use it, would she?

She nodded, murmured, "Yes, I have your number," then opened her door and left the truck. She already felt as if she missed Eli. That was a sensation she was just going to have to get over.

On Thanksgiving Day, Hadley felt a bit nervous about the announcement she was going to make. Brooks Smith was complicating her life, and she was letting him. But the real complication could be her family's reaction to all of it.

Her parents had arrived from Bozeman last night along with her uncle and aunt Jerry and Barbara Strickland. Her mom, Melba and Barbara had had their heads together going over recipes since then. The smells emanating from the kitchen today were worth all of their planning. The boardinghouse was practically bursting at the seams. Somehow they'd all managed to sit in one room for dinner.

There was her grandmother and grandfather, of course, along with her sister Claire, her husband, Levi, and daughter Bekka. Her sister Tessa, her husband, Carson, and their twins, Declan and Charlotte. Jerry and Barbara and their son Trey and his wife, Kayla, and little Gil, too. All Hadley had to do was look at Kayla and she saw her brother Eli's features, the sparkling eyes and the wide smile. Around the table were also Jerry and Barbara's four unmarried sons, Drew, Benjamin, Luke and Billy.

The male cousins talked sports, while the females shared gossip and Old Gene joked with Carson and the twins. The conversation was lively and loud, but it didn't stop Hadley from hearing the question that she dreaded. The one that was always bound to come up when a group like this gathered.

"And who's going to get married next?" her sister Tessa asked.

Old Gene shook his finger at Tessa. "The bigger question is—who's going to produce the next grandchild?"

Luke gave Benjamin a shove in the ribs, but Benjamin just shook his head. Everyone seemed to take the ribbing in stride until Drew said, "Miss All-Business Hadley is more likely to give us grand dogs than grand-babies, don't you think?"

Hadley flashed back to a time when she'd planned to announce her Las Vegas wedding to the whole family. She had been so happy. But her dreams and her hopes had all been a terrible delusion.

Now smiling at everyone, she said, "Grand dogs or grand kitties I can produce. I can probably find one of each for all of you to adopt."

There were groans around the table. Billy said, "As if there's room for an animal in this house."

"There's always room for a pet," Hadley insisted.

Kayla nodded and backed her up. She held

up her hand and said, "Even my brother has adopted a cat and a kitten. Who would have thought? That was all Hadley's doing."

"She can be persuasive when she wants to be," Old Gene said with a wink at her.

Before her family entered territory where she and Eli were lumped together, or before anyone else mused about her romantic life, she passed the serving dish of mashed potatoes to Drew and said, "I have an announcement to make."

"You're engaged," Carson joked.

"Nothing like that," she was quick to assure them all. Then she thought of something. Maybe she should have talked to Old Gene and her grandmother before she announced this to everybody. But it was too late now.

To Melba she said, "I probably should have asked you about this first. Do you mind if I stay a little longer?"

Her mother gave her a look. "Longer? Why would you do that?" Donna Strickland asked her.

Melba, on her other side, patted her hand. "Of course we don't mind if you stay. *If* there's a good reason," she added.

"I think it's a good reason, but you can

judge. I think you know Brooks Smith's dad is recovering from knee-replacement surgery. After Dr. Wellington left, Brooks thought he could handle the practices on his own, but it's become overwhelming at times. So he asked me if I'd stay on the next couple of weeks to help him out. His dad's recovering slowly, and he doesn't want him to rush it."

"But what about your job at the clinic in Bozeman?" her dad asked.

"I spoke with them last night. They tell me as long as I'm back there mid-December, they're fine with me staying here and helping. They brought on a new vet tech, and she's working out well."

"She can't replace you," Hadley's mother insisted.

"True, but it will do me good to get more experience here with horses and cattle. So, Grandmother, if you don't mind my staying—"

Old Gene cut in. "We don't mind at all. It's a shame you can't stay for Christmas."

"Oh, but we'll be glad to have her back in Bozeman," Hadley's mother assured them. "We have to share her, you know."

Everyone around the table laughed. On her other side, Drew leaned close to her and said in a low voice, "I was talking to Derek Dalton at the Ace in the Hole."

"And?" Hadley asked, with a lift of her brow.

"And he said you and Eli Dalton got cozy. You stayed overnight there, and you two were alone in the barn."

"In a cold barn in a blizzard," she reminded him. "We were practically strangers, Drew. Nothing was going to happen overnight. Derek's imagination is too vivid."

"And maybe you're protesting a little too much."

Maybe she was protesting because she could still remember the feel of her head on Eli's shoulder as they cuddled together for warmth. Maybe she was protesting too much because the touch of Eli's lips on hers was more than a memory.

Drew gave her a curious look, then shrugged. "Did Derek ask you on a date and you turned him down?"

"No, we never quite got to that. He approached me at Kayla's wedding and tried to charm me."

"But you can't be charmed?" Drew asked.

"Not by Derek."

"Ah. Could that leave an opening for his older brother?"

She elbowed Drew in the ribs. "Fill your face with that turkey and stop making up scenarios about my life."

Drew behaved for the most part after that, and the conversations jumped around to other things besides marriage and grandchildren.

As she was helping Melba clear the table, Melba said, "You know you're welcome here whenever you want to stay, especially in the winter when we don't have many guests."

Hadley was still smiling at that when the phone on her belt buzzed. In Bozeman she was used to it buzzing all the time—either a client calling or one of the other vets or one of her friends. But here, her phone had mostly been quiet except for texts between her and her sisters.

When she checked the screen now, her heart sped up. It was Eli.

"Hey," she said when she answered, trying to sound casual.

"Hey, yourself. Happy Thanksgiving."

"Happy Thanksgiving to you, too." After she said it, she mentally groaned. How lame could she get?

"You probably have a houseful there at Strickland's."

"We do," she said, sounding a little weary of it.

He chuckled. "A little too much family?"

"I love them all," she reminded him.

He chuckled again. "How would you like to drive over here and have dessert with me in my cabin?"

"I'd like that," she said. "Believe me, nobody here will miss me."

"I doubt that. About half an hour?"

"See you soon." After she ended the call, Hadley wondered what she'd just done. Agreed to a date of sorts?

Tessa was passing by her on the way to the kitchen when Hadley snagged her arm. "I'm going out for a while."

"Out where?" Tessa asked.

"To the Dalton ranch."

"Checking on that foal?" Tessa asked with a twinkle in her eye.

"Sure am," Hadley said with a straight face.

"I'll cover for you," Tessa agreed, then added, "Say hello to Eli for me," and disappeared into the kitchen.

As Hadley went to fetch her coat, she wondered if Eli would be glad she was staying longer in Rust Creek Falls.

She'd soon find out.

Chapter 9

Eli watched for Hadley's SUV. When she drove up and parked near the cabin, he opened his door. He'd debated about calling her. Should he or shouldn't he? He'd asked himself more than once if he wanted more than a casual relationship with her. Hadley was different from any woman he'd dated. She was natural, no fake airs. Animals were more important to her than makeup. Not that she needed makeup. She had a natural beauty that drew him to her. Yes, she'd be returning to Bozeman, but did that really matter if they wanted to see each other?

He'd thought again about Elaine...about her

leaving. Was he really going to let that affect his relationships for the rest of his life? The failure of his first serious relationship had kept him from becoming involved for years.

He'd told himself that today could be the last chance to see Hadley before she left Rust Creek Falls. That conclusion had led him to pick up his phone and call her.

Now Hadley hurried up the walk, saying, "Aren't you afraid the cats will run out?"

"They're sleeping up in the loft," he said, pointing in that direction. "I just got back from the barn checking on Amber and the foal. Come on in."

After Hadley stepped inside, he closed the door. "Are you interested in dessert or sitting in front of the fire?"

"Both sound nice," she admitted.

He went to the fireplace, where he'd laid kindling. Pulling a log from the carrier on the hearth, he placed it in position. "Did you have a nice Thanksgiving with your family?" he asked as she shrugged out of her jacket.

He went to her, and as he took her jacket from her, his fingers brushed hers. When both of them stopped and gazed into each other's eyes, Eli felt the world spin a bit. To find his bearings again, he carried her coat into the kitchen and hung it over one of the chairs. Returning to her, he waited for her answer.

"It was nice," she said, not giving any further explanation.

He never knew how much to prod her, so he said casually, "That doesn't sound like an endorsement for a big family gathering."

With a sigh, Hadley sank down onto the sofa. "The truth is, I needed an excuse to get away."

He could take that as an insult, but he chose not to. If she felt he was a haven of sorts, so be it.

She must have realized what she said. "I'm sorry. I didn't mean to make that sound— I mean, I wanted to come here and have dessert with you."

If he went to her now, he might just take her in his arms and kiss her. That could send her driving back to her family. Instead he put another log on the fire, then he took the can of long matches from the mantel and plucked one out.

"So tell me why you needed an excuse to leave."

"When I'm sitting there with everyone, I feel the pressure of family expectations," she explained.

Eli glanced at her over his shoulder and saw the serious expression on her face. Whatever was bothering her seemed like more than just the typical irritation of family poking into private lives. He kept quiet to see if she'd tell him more.

By the time he'd lit the fire, she'd started talking again.

"I'm aware that my grandmother and my mother think I should settle down and start a family. And maybe that *is* on my mind, too. But that doesn't mean I should want to date every eligible bachelor. That doesn't mean I should jump at the chance of marriage."

A quaver in Hadley's voice alerted Eli, but there was hurt behind her words. He wished she'd confide more in him. However, he saw her lips set perfectly now, and he sensed she was already regretting she'd said too much. He was glad when the cats chose that moment to descend the stairs from the loft. Both of them came running over to Hadley and wrapped around her legs.

Her smile was back as she picked up Winks. "You are such a cutie." She snuggled her until the kitten started squirming.

When she put her down, Winks scrambled

over to Eli and, as before, started climbing up his jean-clad leg.

He caught her at his knee and lifted her into his arms. "She's a character. It's a good thing I don't have curtains on the windows or she'd be climbing them." There was just a Western-patterned valance over each window that had been Kristen's idea. Now he was glad of it.

"You'll have to get them a scratching post and train them to use it, then they won't bother your furniture."

"I'll do that," he said. "So tell me what kind of dessert you'd like. Mom didn't take it all along to Uncle Ben's."

"Why are you here when they're all over there?"

"I just came back to check on the horses and the cats. Believe me, there are enough people there that they won't miss me. Anyway I have apple and pumpkin pies."

"Your mom made you two pies?"

"My cousins drop in. Besides, she knows I like late-night snacks."

Hadley looked up at him and then at the table in the kitchen. "Do you want me to come to the kitchen?"

"No need. We can sit here and enjoy the fire."

She peered into the fire as if she was looking for answers to a question. But then she nodded to him. "I'd like a slice of apple."

"Coming right up. Coffee with that?"

"Sounds good."

From the kitchen, Eli watched her. She was dressed in a green sweater with a black turtleneck underneath. Her slim-cut black jeans showed off her legs above her shoe boots. He saw that she busied herself with the cats while he cut two slices of pie and poured coffee into mugs. He brought it all to the coffee table.

When he sat beside her, they ate. He noticed their silence was companionable and not at all awkward.

After Hadley was finished, she set her dish on the coffee table and let out a sigh. "You know, this is the first I've really relaxed since I got here. The boardinghouse is more like a dorm with everybody in and out of each other's rooms. There's lots of company for meals, and generally speaking I like that."

"Except, sometimes you want private time," Eli guessed.

"Exactly. Private time with no one butting into my business or asking where I'm going or what I'm going to be doing. You'd think I'd be used to it with two sisters. But somehow

I thought once we were adults on our own, that would change."

"That's why I built this house," Eli said with complete understanding. "It was time. My mother gives me the same lecture that your grandmother gives you. That look and a wink that says she wants grandkids from me. And I tell her that will happen when it's supposed to happen."

Somehow while eating their pie and drinking their coffee and talking about family issues they both understood, they had leaned closer to each other. Eli was reading the signals from Hadley that she was glad to be here and glad to be close to him. Yet he sensed her reserve also and wondered if he could break through it.

So instead of wondering, he asked, "Are you going to run if I kiss you again? Or will you stay for a second cup of coffee?"

He thought she swallowed hard. He thought the color in her cheeks pinkened. She hesitated only a moment before she answered him. "I'll stay for the coffee."

He didn't rush and he didn't move too quickly. He realized in some ways he was treating Hadley like a skittish colt. But what other way was there to gentle somebody you wanted to care for? He laid his hand on her shoulder, then he leaned in and rubbed his cheek against hers.

It must have been the right thing to do because she turned her face up to him. When he took her lips, they were soft and welcoming, and he felt as if they'd been building to this since the first moment she'd stepped into his barn. Their other kisses had been impulsive and maybe even considered mistakes by Hadley. But this one was fully consensual.

In no time at all, with his arm wrapped around her, he'd brought her over onto his lap, where kissing was easier. She seemed as lost in him as he was in her. She ran her fingers in his hair and along his jawline. He'd learned restraint in his thirty-plus years, but Hadley's response made him want to break free of all restraints. He'd moved his hand to her breast and was about to take them a little farther when suddenly Whisper jumped up to the back of the sofa.

Eli could tell Hadley was aware of it. Her hand suddenly went to his chest, and she leaned away from him.

In a husky voice, he asked, "Too much?"

"Too fast. I'm not going to let attraction sweep me away into regret."

He had a feeling there was more to those words than the subject of their kiss.

Where they hadn't been awkward before, now they were. He wasn't sure the best way to handle Hadley or the situation.

She slid from his lap back onto the sofa. As he tried to convince his heart to slow, Hadley righted her clothes. But then she turned toward him, one leg up on the sofa, purpose on her pretty face.

Uh-oh. He had a premonition he wasn't going to like what was coming.

Earnestly, she asked, "Why did you stop traveling and rock climbing?"

He'd been right. He didn't like the question, or the answers it brought with it. On the other hand, he realized in order to earn Hadley's trust, he needed to give his. To give himself a moment to pull his thoughts together, he reached up on the sofa to stroke the cat. "I was serious about a woman once... maybe too young to know what serious was or simply too young to read character well. I suppose I ignored things I shouldn't have because she liked to go rock climbing with me. We traveled together. I suppose it was her adventurous spirit I liked. But it was her adventurous spirit or her wanting something bigger that took her away from me. I didn't realize until it was too late that she had no desire to stay in Rust Creek Falls. I didn't realize that what I considered an adventurous spirit in Elaine was really ambition. I thought we were happy. I was wrong. She informed me she felt trapped. So we broke up and I lost the traveling bug."

"And the rock climbing?"

With a shrug, he explained, "I poured that energy into the ranch, making it a success, making sure no one could fault the fencing or the upkeep on the barn or feeding the cattle in winter or making sure the horses had the right feed. Derek might think he's a rancher, but he's not about ranching. Do you know what I mean?"

Her eyes sparkling with empathy, she told him, "I know some vets who are great clinicians, but they don't have a bond with animals."

"I feel the ranch in my blood, just like my father does."

Suddenly there was a loud rap-rap-rap on Eli's door. The next moment the door opened and Derek strode in.

When he saw the two of them on the sofa, he grinned. "Am I interrupting something?"

Before Eli could give him a gruff *turn around and go back outside*, Hadley motioned to their coffee and plates. "Just having dessert."

Derek had never been good at taking hints, and now he didn't take the one that the two of them possibly wanted to be alone. He said, "You have the pies Mom baked." He crossed to the kitchen as if he might steal one.

"You didn't get enough dessert at Uncle Ben's?" Eli asked him.

"I got dessert, but Mom's apple pie went first, and I see you still have some left. Coffee, too. I'll just join you."

There was a retort on the tip of Eli's tongue, but Derek was his brother. He wouldn't get into a spat with him in front of Hadley.

In no time at all, Derek had cut himself a big slice of pie, poured a mug of coffee and sat in the armchair across from the sofa. He said to Eli, "Anderson wanted to know if you want to meet up tomorrow night at the Ace in the Hole. I told him you would."

Eli's cousin Anderson was probably his best friend. Meeting up with him to share a beer and talk sports would be good. "I'll text him later," Eli said. "But that should be okay."

In between forkfuls of pie, Derek asked

Hadley, "Are you going to the holiday dance at the community center on Saturday night?"

"I haven't decided," she said.

"I'd be glad to take you," Derek offered.

"Not necessary, bro. Hadley said if she goes, she's going with me."

Derek looked from one of them to the other. Then he waved his hand across the coffee table. "So this isn't just *we're going to have dessert together*. This is, *we might be dating each other*."

Eli didn't want to put Hadley in the position she didn't want to be in. "I think this is none of your business," Eli said firmly.

Hadley turned around to Winks, who'd fallen asleep on the back of the sofa with her mom. She said, "The cats look great. You're taking wonderful care of them." Then she got to her feet. "I'd better be getting back. My mom and dad will be leaving in the morning, and they'll want to visit while they're here."

That sounded odd to Eli since Hadley would be going back to Bozeman soon. But he'd let her use the excuse. He went to get her coat and helped her put it on. The touch of her hair on his fingers reminded him how soft it was, how much he liked running his fingers through it.

He pointed to Derek. "Don't eat all the pie. I'm going to walk Hadley out."

His brother gave him a thumbs-up.

As soon as they were outside, Hadley turned to him. "You don't have to feel obligated to go with me to the dance. I know you were just protecting me from Derek."

"Nope, I wasn't. I know you don't need protection. Asking you to go with me has nothing to do with him."

"You didn't exactly ask," she teased.

"Well, I'm asking you now. Will you go to the dance with me?"

"I will," she said with a wide smile.

He couldn't help it then. He had to kiss her again.

They created enough heat to ward off the cold, but once again Hadley pulled away. "I really do need to get back. The reason I need to spend time with my parents tonight is that I won't be seeing them again for a couple of weeks."

He waited for her to explain.

"Brooks asked me to stay and help him, and that's what I'm going to do. I cleared it with my practice."

"So the dance at the community center might not be our first and last date?"

"Might not," she said coyly. Then she gave him a wave and went to her SUV.

Eli felt as if he'd just been handed an early Christmas present. Now he just had to figure out what to do with it.

On Friday, Eli pulled a hay bale from the back of the buckboard and laid it out for the cattle. His mind was on another viewing party tonight at the Ace in the Hole. He was going to meet his cousin Anderson there. Would Hadley be there, too? He couldn't wait for the dance tomorrow night to see her again.

Thinking about holding her in his arms, he came back to earth when his dad asked from the driver's seat of the buckboard, "Need a hand?" His father had a weathered face and dark brown hair heavily laced with gray. He usually wore his hat, so not many people noticed he was going bald on top. Eli had looked up to him all of his life and liked working beside him.

"I'm fine," Eli called back. This wasn't like him not to keep his mind on what he was doing. After he finished with a few of the bales, he climbed back in the buckboard to take the feed a little farther. This was a good time to talk to his dad about something.

"What do you think would please Mom for Christmas?"

His father just shook his head. "She insists she doesn't need anything, so I don't know what to tell you. Maybe you should get some advice from that woman you have your eye on."

Eli was surprised his dad had noticed.

Surprising him again, his dad went on, "Your mom thinks that girl has her head on straight."

"Hadley's a very caring vet."

"Um," his dad mumbled, "that's about her job. What about *her*?"

Eli and his dad talked straight when they talked serious. "I think somebody did a number on her."

"You mean like Elaine did to you?"

There again Eli didn't think his dad had paid all that much attention. After all, Eli had tried to hide his feelings about the breakup, about the disappointment he felt in not having the future he'd envisioned. Apparently his father saw more than Eli realized.

"Yeah, just like that," he answered. "The other thing is—she's college educated. She's getting her pilot's license. I think she wants to own her own practice someday."

"And you mind you didn't go to college?"

"No, it's not that I mind. I didn't want it. I didn't think I needed it."

"You feel less than her?" his dad asked perceptively. "You know, if you want a college education you can do it on that computer of yours."

Eli had thought about that, too, getting a degree that way. Something in business management, maybe, that would help him run the ranch.

His phone inside his coat pocket vibrated and buzzed. It was the signal that a text had come in. Cell service could be spotty out here but texts usually made their way through. Slipping it from his pocket he saw that it was from Derek. The text made fear grip Eli's chest. 911.

Eli knew Derek had gone out snowmobiling on the other side of the ranch. Keeping his voice as calm as he could, he said to his father, "We've got to head back. Derek could be in trouble."

As Hadley entered the boardinghouse, bags in hand, she realized she hadn't gone dress shopping in way too long. She actually had had fun, and she'd found something for the dance that might make Eli take a second look tomorrow night, and maybe even a third.

She entered the kitchen to hopefully pull Claire upstairs with her so she could show her the dress. But then Claire's husband, Levi, came clomping down the stairs and into the kitchen, his cell phone at his ear, worry on his face. Into the phone he said, "I'll load up Old Gene's snowmobile on his truck. Be there in ten."

"What's wrong?" Claire asked.

"An alarm has been sounded for anyone with a snowmobile."

"What happened?" Hadley asked.

"Derek is missing. He went out snowmobiling and texted Eli a 911 message. Nothing since then."

Levi grabbed his jacket from the peg near the door but Hadley called to him. "I'm going with you." She dropped her bags on the counter and asked Claire, "Will you take these up to my room?" Then she was hurrying after Levi, praying nothing serious had happened to the brother Eli loved.

At the Circle D, Hadley raced into the house while Levi unloaded the snowmobile and spoke to other ranchers who had gathered there. In the kitchen Rita Dalton was busy making sandwiches while two coffee-pots brewed.

Hadley shrugged out of her coat. "What can I do to help?"

"They started the search about an hour ago. Eli's been out there the longest. The searchers are going to need sandwiches and coffee to keep them going. Can you fill those thermoses? Just add a touch of milk. Most of the men like it that way."

"You've done this before," Hadley guessed.

"I had lots of experience after the flood. Now once in a while we get a lost hiker. Before I've never had to worry that one of my own was out there, possibly hurt." Rita's voice cracked.

Hadley went to her and put her arm around the woman's shoulders. She didn't say anything because she realized Rita was a realistic woman who didn't want platitudes. They didn't know what had happened to Derek or what would happen next.

After a moment, Rita pulled away. She continued to assemble sandwiches. Then she said, "A rancher's wife has to be prepared for anything." Her gaze met Hadley's, and there seemed to be a message in that. She went on. "All I ever wanted was to be a wife and a mom. That single focus has driven my life, and there hasn't been room for much else. But now that my children are grown, my girls and Jonah married, Eli with his own house, I respect women with careers even more. They have something else to occupy their thoughts when their children are on their own. That might make for livelier conversation with their husbands."

Hadley said, "It's never too late to have other interests."

"Oh, Charles and I are set in our ways. But you might have a point. I might stop in at the community center and see if anyone's interested in organizing a book club or something like that."

Hadley had poured coffee into the thermoses and was making sandwiches with Rita when Charles tramped in the door. "Eli found Derek. He's bringing him home."

"Is Derek hurt?" Rita asked.

"We don't know what condition he's in," Charles answered her. "Eli didn't say. I've called the paramedics just in case. Even if the boy is on his feet, something happened out there and I want him checked out."

Rita nodded her approval at that.

The paramedics arrived before Eli. Hadley

went outside to wait. The revolving red light on the paramedic's van cast an eerie glow over the snow. She heard the sound of a snowmobile before she saw it. Then she saw the machine and the man driving it, and Derek holding on behind Eli. If he was holding on, he had to be all right. At least that's what she told herself, though she didn't know for sure.

She stayed back as Rita and Charles crowded around their sons. The paramedics took control, spoke with Eli and handled Derek as if he were glass. They laid him on a board, put a collar around his neck and then loaded him into the ambulance.

They were backing out, when Eli saw her. "What are you doing here?"

"I had to know if you were okay…if Derek was okay."

The features of his face softened a bit. "I have to follow the ambulance to the hospital."

"I'll go with you," she said impulsively. "Let me grab coffee and a couple of sandwiches for you."

"No need," he said, raising his hand. But she didn't listen. She ran to the house, grabbed the items and ran to Eli's truck that he'd already started up. She hopped inside before he could protest.

"Hadley, there's going to be a lot of waiting."

"I know that. Don't you need someone to wait with you?"

He cut her a glance and turned up the heater. She realized he had to be freezing from being out in that weather for the time he'd been searching. It probably hadn't been easy finding Derek in the snow, getting him on the machine and worrying through the ride back.

Without being asked, she poured coffee into the top cup of the thermos. "Take this," she said, "and drink it."

He didn't argue. After he swallowed about half the coffee, he handed it back to her.

"Just tell me if you want more. How about a sandwich?"

He shook his head. "Maybe later."

"Do you want to talk about it?"

Eli seemed to mull that over. "I was never so scared as when I got that text from him. It was just '911' then it cut out. I tried calling him back. I tried texting him back. But there was no answer. I think he passed out. He probably has a concussion and maybe a broken arm. I don't know how he held on to me on the way back, but he insisted that we do it that way. I wasn't going to argue. I just wanted to get him warmed up."

"What happened?"

"I think he hit an ice patch. I found him pinned under the machine. But once I moved the snowmobile off him, he insisted he was perfectly capable of riding back with me. I'm still afraid I made the wrong decision. But with the snow and night falling, I didn't have any choice."

She reached over and touched Eli's arm. If he had more to say, she'd let him get it out.

"I'd had some first aid training. I checked his breathing and took his pulse. But nothing prepares you for an emergency like that. Absolutely nothing."

"Your mom was worried sick about both of you, but she didn't let it show much."

"That's Mom. I'm so thankful for everyone who came out to search. I think every man in town who had a snowmobile came to the ranch."

"Levi included. That's how I knew what had happened."

"That's the emergency alert chain. One person calls the next."

"Rust Creek Falls is really a tight-knit community," she mused.

"Yes, it is. Neighbors really care about each other."

"Not just neighbors," she said lightly.

Eli cut her another glance.

What had she just admitted? That she cared about Eli Dalton?

As if he wasn't sure what she'd meant either, he said, "I'll take more of that coffee now."

She added hot coffee to what was already in the cup, handed it to him and watched his large, capable hands as he drank the coffee and expertly steered the truck. When she couldn't tear her gaze from him, she knew then without a doubt she was falling for Eli Dalton.

What was she going to do about that?

Chapter 10

Hadley didn't try to make conversation as she and Eli sat in the hospital waiting room for over an hour. Eli had alternated between pacing, sitting and brooding. Talking would have been too much of a burden at a time like this.

Finally she looked at the thermos that she'd brought inside with her. "How about another cup of coffee? I'm sure it's better than what's in any vending machine here."

Eli glanced over at her as if he were seeing her for the first time. "Thanks for coming along and waiting with me. If I don't call

Mom and Dad with some kind of report soon, they're going to be here, too."

"Evaluation and tests take time," Hadley reminded him.

"I'm sure this isn't the way you expected to spend your evening," he muttered.

"I've learned life often takes twists and turns I don't expect." She couldn't help but think about what happened with Justin and what a scoundrel he'd been. She'd been a terrible judge of character because she'd been blinded by attraction. She'd sworn to herself that would never happen again. This attraction to Eli had thrown her into a tizzy because she needed to see through it to the real man underneath.

Suddenly the doctor appeared in the doorway. Eli stood and so did Hadley.

The doctor nodded to Hadley. "Is she family?"

Eli didn't hesitate to say, "Close enough."

The doctor didn't question him. "Your brother has a concussion. His arm is badly sprained but not broken. He'll have to wear a sling. He's protesting that he wants to leave. He can, of course, sign himself out, but it would be better if you convince him to stay overnight for observation."

"I'll try to do that," Eli said, looking somewhat relieved. "But he can be stubborn."

"Young men his age often are. Come on, I'll show you to his cubicle."

"Do you want me to come?" Hadley asked.

Eli didn't hesitate. "Yes. We might need two against one."

Their gazes met, and Hadley saw more than a common purpose in Eli. She felt her nerve endings light up. Even in these circumstances, the attraction between them pulled like a strong magnet. Eli might have his brother on his mind, but when he looked at her, she could feel the bond that had formed between them. And not only the bond. She couldn't deny the fact that she wanted to be held in his arms again, wanted to feel another kiss, wanted to kiss him back and maybe more. She'd guarded herself for so long, but somehow Eli had broken through that guard, not forcefully, but gently and persuasively.

He reached for her hand then as they walked toward Derek's cubicle. Seeing the man underneath the sexy rancher, she realized that there was so much strength in Eli. She could feel the calluses on his fingers from hard work. But more than that, she felt his warmth. She felt the energy that invigorated her in a way she hadn't been invigorated before. Just what was it about this tall rancher that made her rethink her past and maybe even her future?

As she walked into Derek's cubicle with Eli, she didn't know what to expect. Certainly not what she found. A pale Derek talking to one of the nurses, smiling at her with that twinkle in his eyes.

The nurse moved away, and he saw them. "Why are you two looking so serious? I'm still alive and I'm ready to go home."

Eli strode over to his brother's bed and Hadley followed him, knowing this could be a battle.

"Don't make light of what happened to you," Eli warned his brother.

"I have a headache the size of the state of Montana. I'm not making light of it," Derek told him. "But my brush with that snowmobile isn't going to make me an invalid either."

"You've got to stay the night," Eli said firmly.

"I don't," Derek protested. "All I have to do is sign a paper and I'm out of here."

Eli threw a glance at Hadley and she stepped into the situation, even though she didn't know if she wanted to. She sank down onto the chair beside Derek's bed. "Let me tell you what happened, Derek."

"I was there. I know what happened," he said, his smile fading.

"You know what happened to *you*, but let me tell you about the rest of the people who care about you. When the call went out that you were missing—"

"I wasn't missing," he mumbled.

"Well, apparently your cell phone was because it didn't answer when Eli or your mom and dad repeatedly tried to call you. Anyone in Rust Creek Falls with a snowmobile rushed to the Circle D, including my brother-in-law. That's how I found out about what was happening. When I arrived, your mom was fluttering around the kitchen like a busy bee trying to hide all her worry. But she couldn't. She was worried sick, and so was everyone else who was gathering for the search. She and I made sandwiches and coffee to distribute to the searchers as they took breaks. You know it *is* cold out there. You're fortunate you didn't get frostbite."

When Derek started to protest, she held up her hand. "Eli was searching the longest, so of course your mom and dad were worried about him, too. With spotty cell phone reception, they couldn't stay in touch. Can you imagine worrying for that hour or two?"

Derek's face showed that, yes, he could.

"As soon as Eli reports to your parents, your mom and dad are going to drive here to make sure you're all right. You're going to prove you are by staying overnight and letting the doctors and nurses fuss over you. Just consider this your chance to acquire a few more females' phone numbers." She arched her brows and waited for Derek's reply.

He glanced at his brother. "She's good."

Eli placed his hand on her shoulder. "I know she is. Why do you think I let her come along?"

She eyed Eli and then Derek. "He didn't *let* me come along. I jumped into his truck before he knew what was happening. He needed the coffee."

Derek laughed out loud. "So you two are a couple. Who would have thought!"

Neither of them responded to that comment.

Eli said, "I want to make that call to Mom and Dad. When I tell them you're going to stay the night, they'll be here as fast as they can."

Derek seemed to regroup, and some of his

bravado faded away. "All right," he said in a resigned tone. "Make the call. I'll stay."

Once Eli had called his mom and dad, it seemed like Charles Dalton must have put the pedal to the metal. They arrived at the hospital in record time. Once Rita was fussing over Derek, Eli gave his brother a wave, took Hadley's arm and said, "I'll let Mom take over now."

On the return drive to Rust Creek Falls, they didn't talk much. Eli switched the radio on to a country channel. As they neared town, Hadley said, "I came to your ranch with Levi. You'll have to drop me at the boardinghouse."

But when Eli reached town, he didn't drive directly to the boardinghouse. He turned off into the parking lot for Wings to Go. He parked in a back corner where the lights weren't too glaring and let the engine idle.

"What are we doing here?" she asked.

"I didn't want to park in front of the boardinghouse and be interrupted by the porch light going on." He unfastened his seat belt and then unfastened hers. "Thank you again for what you did with Derek. I don't think I could have convinced him to stay at the hospital overnight."

"Sure, you could have. You're an older brother. You would have bribed him."

Eli laughed out loud at that one. "Maybe I could have, but he's as stubborn as my dad."

"And probably as stubborn as you."

"I'm only stubborn when I'm right," he insisted.

"I'm sure Derek and your dad think the same thing."

She could see only the shadow of Eli's face, but she thought she saw his lips twitch up.

"We still have a date tomorrow night, don't we?" he asked.

"We do. I even bought a dress."

He tilted his head. "That isn't a weekly occurrence?"

"I haven't had much occasion to get dressed up lately."

"Sometime, Hadley Strickland, you're going to tell me what you're *not* telling me."

Panic assaulted her. She certainly couldn't tell Eli what she'd never even told her family. And what good would it do if she was going back to Bozeman? He certainly wouldn't be leaving Rust Creek Falls.

"Do you think you know me so well?" she asked lightly.

"Oh, I'm beginning to know you well. Very

well," he murmured as he leaned closer to her. Suddenly she realized she didn't want to be interrupted by a porch light either. She wanted Eli's kiss. It wasn't like they could do more than that here in the parking lot in the cold. At least not very much more.

When Eli nudged her chin up, she felt him wait a beat as if asking if she wanted this, too. Yes, she did. As he bent his head and set his lips on hers, she knew this wouldn't be a simple kiss. Whenever Eli kissed, he was all male, all passion, all masterful intensity. Their kiss took her thoughts as easily as it took her breath.

As his tongue searched her mouth, she felt the fire. He kissed her deeply, and she felt as if she were flying solo into the wild blue yonder. There wasn't any other exhilaration like it. His arm dropped down to her back to bring her closer, and closer was what she wanted to be. She ran her fingers up the nape of Eli's neck and felt him shudder. Apparently she had the same power over him that he had over her. A kiss or a touch, and she could go up in flames. Did he feel that way? Even with Justin, she hadn't felt this kind of sexual hunger. It almost shocked her. But then she realized how selfish Justin's lovemaking had been. After the fact, she realized how selfish his life had been.

Why did the thought of Justin always have to interfere?

Eli deepened the kiss, and she almost forgot where her thoughts had been going. Why couldn't she just give in to this?

Because she was too scared to trust her own judgment?

He pulled back and said huskily, "Not a porch light this time."

Although for a while conscious thought had fled, it had returned with a vengeance. Eli had realized her mind had gone somewhere else. She saw it on his face.

"I'm sorry," she said.

He gently touched her cheek and ran his thumb down her chin. "There's nothing to be sorry about. This is a two-way street. And speaking of streets, I'd better get you home before the whole town closes down for the night."

He was treating the end of their kiss nonchalantly, and she didn't know if she wanted him to. Before he could fasten his seat belt, she leaned over and kissed his cheek.

"What was that for?" he asked.

"For not pushing."

"I'm pushing for our date tomorrow night. I'm looking forward to it. Pick you up at seven?"

"That sounds good."

He shifted his truck into Drive and drove out of the parking lot onto the deserted streets. When he pulled up in front of the boardinghouse, the porch light was already on.

"Somebody wanted to give you a guiding light home," he said.

"Levi's been home for hours. I texted Claire from the hospital, but that doesn't mean they all won't worry."

When she reached for the door handle, Eli leaned toward her much as she had done to him. He gave her a gentle kiss on the temple. "Sleep well, Hadley."

After she hopped out of his truck and started up the steps to the boardinghouse, she looked back over her shoulder and could see his shadow there. She had a feeling she'd sleep a lot better in his arms.

When Eli came to the boardinghouse to pick up Hadley on Saturday evening, he absolutely took her breath away. He was dressed in a Western-cut sports jacket with a white shirt, bolo tie and black jeans and boots. His black Stetson was cocked at the angle she liked best. She was immediately taken back to their phone conversation that morning. She'd called him to find out how Derek was doing. He'd responded with, "Do you know how many girls have called to ask how he is?"

She'd laughed and said, "I'm just inquiring because I know you'll feel better when he's home. Any word from the hospital?"

"Derek should be discharged this afternoon. Mom will cluck over him until he can't stand it. Then he'll escape to my place to get away from her care."

"I bet she'll bake extra goodies for both of you."

"There *are* some benefits," he'd said with some amusement, and his voice had gone husky when he said again, "I'm so looking forward to dancing with you tonight."

Now here he was, looking at her as if he'd never seen a woman in a dress before. She'd bought the dress because she felt pretty in it. It had tight long sleeves, a slim waist, a floaty short skirt and, above all, it was red. She didn't know how long the two of them stared at each other.

All of a sudden Old Gene appeared and clapped Eli on the back. "Melba and I thought about going to the dance, but we're taking care of the young-uns."

Melba had slipped up beside Hadley and now she handed her her coat. "You're going to need this, I think." Hadley felt foolish, like a schoolgirl lost in a dream or her first date.

Eli took the coat from her hands and held it for her as she put it on. When she turned to face him, he said in a low voice, "You look beautiful."

She'd heard those words before from another man's lips. But this was Eli, and the look in his eyes said he meant them.

He held her arm as they descended the steps, then helped her up into his truck. On the short drive to the community center, he asked, "So your sisters will be here tonight?"

"Tessa and Carson are busy. Claire and Levi are coming. Ever since they solidified their marriage and renewed their commitment to each other, they try to get out more."

"And Old Gene and Melba help with that?"

"They do. It's nice to see."

"I guess after kids come, still maintaining date nights keeps a marriage strong."

"I suppose it does."

At the community center, Eli parked and then came around the truck for her. He helped her down and made sure he held her arm tightly in case there were any icy spots to walk over. She hadn't wanted to wear her boots with this dress, opting for heels.

Once inside, he took her coat for her and hung it on the rack. They wandered into the main room, where the dance was being held.

Brooks and Jazzy waved to them from one of the tables. "Would you like to sit with them?" Hadley asked.

"Sure, let's."

She could feel Eli's hand at the small of her back as he guided her to the table. She liked the feel of his strength and his tall figure beside her.

After they were seated, Brooks said to her, "Just the person I wanted to see."

Jazzy nudged his arm. "You're not going to talk business, are you?"

"I thought we might as well get it out of the way first, then we can enjoy the rest of the night."

Hadley looked at him with questioning eyes. "What business?"

"I just want to say again how glad I am you're going to stay to help out with my practice."

"I'm glad to do it. But I have to be back

mid-December to cover for my boss. Especially on Christmas Day."

"I understand," Brooks said, shaking his head. "But I wanted to tell you that my dad's made a decision. He's going to put his practice and his property up for sale. I wanted you to be the first to know."

"Are you sure this is a good time for him to make that decision?" Hadley asked. "Maybe he's just frustrated he's not getting better quicker."

"I said the same thing," Brooks admitted. "But he seems pretty sure of himself. He says he'll continue to help me however he can, but he won't have the administrative headaches. He won't have the ranch to care for. I think he's found he likes being under the same roof as we are. It gives him a feeling of security. Going forward, that's important for him."

"When is he going to close his practice?"

"He won't do anything official until spring, but I just wanted you to know."

So now she knew. But she wasn't sure what it meant for her, if anything.

A DJ up at the front of the room had started the music. A buffet line was forming, and Eli asked, "Do you want to get something to eat?"

"I do," she said, not wanting to think about the future tonight.

During the meal of pulled pork, barbecued beef, twice-baked potatoes, raw veggies and more, they easily chatted with Brooks and Jazzy.

Jazzy filled them in on what had happened on *The Great Roundup* episode last night.

Jazzy explained, "Brenna and Summer were paired up. They had to get two cows and calves off of an island in the middle of the pond! And then, after they swam back to shore, Summer, who's a flirt, attacked Brenna for being *little miss perfect*. They actually had a girl fight in the mud!"

Brooks was grinning. "I wish I could have seen that."

Hadley knew Brooks had taken his snowmobile to the Circle D to search for Derek, too. Eli's arm brushed hers, and their eyes met for a brief second.

Eli broke the eye contact first and asked Jazzy, "So who won last night?"

With a wide smile, Jazzy proclaimed, "Brenna did. Not only the fight but the challenge."

"And what did she win?" Hadley asked.

"A romantic night for two at the lodge with

dinner. She took Trav as her date," Jazzy answered.

Although there was lightness on the surface of their conversation, Hadley felt the undercurrent every time her arm brushed Eli's, every time they glanced each other's way, every time they reached for a dish and their fingers touched. There was a raw sexuality surrounding Eli that drew her closer without him saying a word or moving a muscle. But when they touched… She imagined Brenna's night at the lodge with Travis and knew that's what she wanted with Eli.

When they'd all finished eating, Eli asked her, "How about a dance?"

Just the idea of being held in Eli's arms made her heart flutter erratically. She said *yes* because this was an adventure she wanted to go on. Nothing too improbable could happen on the dance floor. She'd be safe from her own impulses and his.

Nevertheless, once he took her into his arms, she rethought that idea. Nothing about being this close to Eli was safe, not when he smelled like a pine woods, not when he looked at her with that smoldering passion in his eyes. Their bodies were just grazing each other, and that was enough to tease her silly.

"I could use your expertise," he said.

At that she studied his face. "My expertise in what?" she asked cautiously.

He grinned. "How about going shopping with me tomorrow to find a Christmas present for my mom? My dad has no idea what she'd like. She says she has everything she needs, so I need a woman's point of view. Maybe you can come up with something I can't."

Looking into Eli's eyes, Hadley almost couldn't think straight. But his words penetrated, and she realized he really was asking her for a favor. She didn't have much opportunity to go shopping, but she enjoyed it when she did. "Sure, I'll go with you," she said. "Just make sure your wallet's full."

He laughed and clasped her a little closer. His fingers encircled hers as he brought her hand to his chest. She took in a breath, suddenly filled with the desire to do more than dance. That desire made her notice everything about him, from his clean-shaven jaw, to his hair dipping over his brow, to the lines around his eyes that came from squinting into the sun…or from laughter. She had a feeling there had been lots of laughter in Eli's life with his brothers and his sisters. He enjoyed his life now, that was obvious.

They navigated around other couples on the dance floor, including Levi and Claire, but Hadley didn't really notice them. She and Eli seemed to be moving in their own world to music soft and sultry meant only for them. At this moment Hadley couldn't imagine being anywhere else.

One dance faded into two, and they molded to each other even more closely. He brushed his cheek against hers, and she wanted to kiss him right then and there. As the dance ended, Eli did place a light kiss on her lips. It was a promise of more to come.

He said close to her ear, "I like dancing with you, but you know what I'd like even more?"

She could hardly get the word out. "What?"

"I want to be alone with you. Will you come back to my place with me?"

She said the only word that was in her head. "Yes."

An hour later, back at his cabin with Hadley, Eli realized all his experience with women hadn't taught him how to handle tonight with Hadley. As they'd danced, he'd been sure she wanted the same thing he did. But she'd gotten very quiet on the drive here. Not that he'd been a chatterbox himself. After all, they knew what they were going to do, didn't they?

Once they'd come inside, he'd taken her coat from her and told her to make herself comfortable. Now she was sitting on the sofa with Winks and Whisper, giving all of her attention to them. She seemed fidgety to him.

Earlier, he'd laid the fire in the fireplace, ready to be set with a flick of a match. Now he did that and watched as the flames took hold. Maybe a little conversation would go a long way. Maybe he could coax her to open up. If she did, he'd know she was ready for whatever tonight brought.

Going to the sofa, he sat beside her. The kitten ran back and forth between their laps, and they both smiled. He settled his arm around her shoulders and brought her close. She didn't resist.

"I read the signals right tonight, didn't I?" he asked. "You wanted to come back here with me?"

She looked up at him, but there was a slight furrow in her brow. "I did want to come back here with you. That's why I said *yes*."

"You don't seem comfortable, though. Are you having doubts? We can just sit by the fire and talk."

She nodded, seeming to agree with him about that. "What do you want to talk about?"

Momma cat and baby settled in a corner of the sofa watching them.

He brushed his fingers down Hadley's arm. He knew what he wanted to ask her. "Why are you willing to work on Christmas, which is a family time?"

That brought a deeper furrow to her brow. She was quiet so long he wasn't sure she was going to answer him. But then she said, "It *is* a family time, and I do enjoy that part of it. But ever since—" She stopped.

"Ever since what?"

"For me the holidays have become associated with disappointment and shame."

He wasn't sure what to say to that. So he stroked her arm again and listened.

"I broke up with my ex the day before Christmas."

"Oh, Hadley, I'm sorry." He couldn't imagine why a man would break up with her. Or had *she* broken it off? "Do you want to tell me what happened?"

"I met Justin at a veterinary convention in

Las Vegas three years ago. He swept me off my feet. He was a pharmaceutical rep with a lot of charm, and I guess I fell for it. It didn't last long," she said.

Being around Hadley as much as he had been, especially having her sleep in his arms with complete vulnerability, Eli realized she still hadn't let her guard down completely. He didn't think she'd given him the whole story, but that story was hers to tell when she trusted him.

"Any man who would walk away from you or let *you* walk away from *him* would have to be some kind of fool," he assured her.

Her cheeks reddened a little, and he saw her eyes tear up. "It was complicated."

"And you still hurt from it."

She nodded.

He held her closer then and swiped away the single tear that was rolling down her cheek. He couldn't keep from kissing her. He knew she wanted that kiss, too, when her arms rounded his neck and her fingers laced in his hair. He'd been anticipating the kiss and longing to take it somewhere else. Yet he knew he couldn't hurry her. He couldn't hurry this. When he leaned back, she moaned a little. He smiled and used his tongue to outline her lips. He could feel her tremble and knew she liked it. He was certain of it when her hand went under his shirt placket and she touched bare skin.

"Hadley," he groaned.

"What?"

"Do you want to take this up to the bedroom?"

She nodded again against his chest. That was the only signal he needed. He swooped her up into his arms, strode to the stairs and carried her up to the loft. They were in a big, king-size bed in no time, and all he wanted to do was strip her clothes off her and rid himself of his. But, again, he didn't want to rush. He didn't know how he could keep from rushing, but that was the plan.

Hadley didn't hesitate now. Her hands went to the buttons on his shirt. She pulled his shirt out of his slacks, and he figured it would give her a measure of confidence for him to disrobe first. So he let her take off his shirt and skim it down his arms. He couldn't help but suck in a breath when she leaned forward and kissed his chest.

He said huskily, "We've got to get your clothes off, too."

"Mine are easier," she said simply. And he

had to laugh. He could see what she meant. There was one zipper down the back of her dress. He didn't even have to turn her around to reach it and pull it down. The dress slipped from her shoulders, and she was standing before him in a bra that seemed a filmy bit of nothing and panties that were the same. They were under her pantyhose, but he could tell. Had she anticipated tonight, too?

"Shoes," he whispered before he peeled them down her hips and then her legs. She held on to his shoulder as he pulled off one foot and then the other and tossed the pantyhose aside.

"The rest of your clothes," she breathed.

Once she had unbuttoned his belt buckle, ridding himself of the rest of his clothes didn't take long at all. In a matter of seconds, they were in his bed and he'd laid a condom on the nightstand.

"Are you on the pill?" he asked.

"No," she said simply, and he suspected what that meant. She hadn't dated recently. She hadn't seen anyone seriously recently. But still he wanted to know. "Have you been involved with anyone since your ex?"

"No."

That meant he was right about going slow.

He was right about taking precious care of her. And he did. Although Hadley was impatient, he kept it slow, and she soon fell into the experience with him, making it more sensual. He kissed her cheek. She kissed his. He kissed her jawline. She kissed his. He kissed her collarbone. She kissed his. And so it went until she was at his waist and he couldn't take it any longer.

Applying the condom first, he rose above her. He stroked her thighs apart and could tell she was ready for him. "I want you, Hadley."

"I want you, Eli."

And so they had each other until he saw stars, she shouted his name…and the whole universe seemed to explode.

Chapter 11

Hadley awakened in Eli's arms. This experience was so different from when they'd awakened in the tack room with all their clothes on. He was cuddling her close, and his chest hair brushed her nose. She felt the tips of his fingers along the crest of her shoulder, and she shivered, remembering everything from last night.

"Are you cold?" he whispered, close to her ear.

"Anything but," she assured him, burrowing her nose into his chest. She'd been free with him last night and so hungry for him. That embarrassed her a bit now.

"What's wrong?" he asked, giving her a look that said he wanted the truth.

"Last night was wonderful." She hurried to explain, "But I've never been quite like that. I just feel a bit embarrassed this morning, that I was so—"

"Sensual? Hungry for me like I was for you? There's nothing wrong with that, Hadley. In fact, that's what made it so electric and…fun."

She poked him in the ribs. "Fun?"

He laughed. "Don't you want to have fun in bed?"

When she thought about Justin, she didn't think about fun. She thought about lust. She thought about chemistry and where that had gotten her. She had chemistry with Eli, that was for sure. But there was more, too, and that's what puzzled her. Her feelings for him were becoming so much more expansive than a simple attraction.

"Your mind's going. I can hear the wheels turning," he teased.

"Stop them from turning," she said.

"Gladly."

When his lips came down on hers, pleasure seemed to fill every bit of her. As his tongue stroked her mouth, she passed her hands down his back, felt the strong muscles there as well as his spine. She raked her nails across his skin, and he groaned. His caresses were more than touches. They were embedded with caring. She felt that as well as the desire to arouse her.

When she stroked his hip, he said, "I have trouble restraining myself around you."

"Maybe we shouldn't think about restraints this morning," she suggested. That caused another groan.

She found herself wanting to look at him as well as touch him. But that was hard to do when he was determined to make her melt. When both of them were panting and glazed with desire, he prepared himself, stretched out on top of her and slowly let their lower bodies touch. It was a teasing ritual that made her frantic to have him. But he wasn't ready to take her yet. He concentrated on her breasts. His mouth on them made her dizzy with need.

She'd never ever felt like this. Last night they'd been seriously sensual and seriously hungry for each other. But this morning, they both tantalized and teased, having some of that fun Eli had mentioned. Finally, finally, he entered her. She took him in, glorying in every sensation. They seemed to melt into each other as heat wrapped them in an embrace. Before she knew it, she was reaching for the same stars she'd claimed last night, only this morning she seemed to reach higher and farther until she felt their glimmer through every nerve ending. Her climax rocked her. She felt his rock him.

Just what did this mean for either of them? She wasn't going to think about that now.

She decided not to think about it two hours later, either, after they showered together, dressed, looked after the horses and driven to Kalispell. The mall was bustling with pre-Christmas activity. They stopped at Santa's Workshop in the middle of the mall, where children and parents lined up so their kids could sit on Santa's knee.

"How many do you want someday?" Eli asked.

She gave him a quick look, but his question had seemed nonchalant as if he was just gathering information.

"Kids? I haven't really thought about it," she said. "I always thought I'd have pets sooner than kids. How about you?"

"Two or three," he answered reasonably.

"Enough that they'd have each other, not too many that they don't get enough attention."

That was a well-thought-out answer. Eli had spent time thinking about it, whereas she hadn't. Because she thought it would never happen? Because trusting a man again had seemed so impossible? When they walked away from the line of children and parents, she had a lot to think about.

They wandered in and out of shops until Hadley spotted something that might be the perfect gift for Rita Dalton. She took Eli's arm and pulled him toward a display of wooden keepsake boxes. One had a beautiful carving of a horse on the lid.

She asked, "Do you think you could coax your brothers and sisters to do something special for your mom?"

"That depends," he said warily. "What would they have to do?"

"What if each of you put a note or letter in here about what she means to you. I can't think of a Christmas gift that would be more appreciated."

Eli first discriminately studied the box. He opened the lid and saw its blue velvet-lined interior. Then his gaze fell on Hadley. "You haven't known my mother very long, but you're right. That would be a very precious gift to her."

"To any mother," Hadley assured him.

"You've found the perfect gift. Now all I have to do is make sure my family cooperates."

"I don't think you'll have a problem with that."

Eli was a leader, and she expected that his brothers and sisters respected him enough to see the wisdom in what he asked.

Hadley's cell phone buzzed. She'd texted Claire this morning and told her where she was and what she'd be doing...for the most part.

Eli said, "Go ahead and answer it. I'll take this up to the counter."

As he carried the box up to the sales clerk, Hadley stepped to a quiet corner and checked the screen on her phone. It wasn't Claire. However, she knew the name on the caller ID. She just hadn't heard from him in a few months. Greg Fordham had gone to vet school with her. The last time she'd heard from him this summer, he'd still been practicing in St. Louis.

She answered, "Hadley Strickland here."

"Hadley, it's Greg."

"Hi. It's been a while." She waited, wondering what he wanted.

"I'm flying into Kalispell tomorrow and I'd like to have dinner with you."

"Dinner? Why?"

He laughed. "That's what I like about you, Hadley. You ask the tough questions. I want to consult with you about something."

"I see," she said, though she really didn't. "I'm working with a vet in Rust Creek Falls while I'm in town."

"I can drive *there* if it's more convenient for you."

She thought about Eli and whether they'd be spending more time together, maybe tomorrow evening.

"There aren't many food choices here, but there's a great rustic place called the Ace in the Hole."

He laughed. "Will I get into a bar fight?"

"Not if you behave yourself."

"All right. That sounds like a plan. What time should I meet you there?"

"About six?" she asked. "If I'm going to be tied up, I'll give you a call back."

"You have my number. I should be getting into Kalispell around noon. I'll text you where I'm staying in case you need that."

"Are you sure you don't want to tell me what this is about?" she asked, still puzzled by his call.

"No, I'd rather discuss it in person. I'll see you tomorrow at the Ace in the Hole."

The call ended and Hadley once more belted her phone. Just what did Greg Fordham want with her?

When Greg walked into the Ace in the Hole, he looked totally out of place. But that wasn't a surprise to Hadley. He was wearing an expensive suit, which he usually did. He came from money and he had a trust fund, but he'd become a veterinarian because he loved animals. Because of that, they had connected.

She stood and waved to him, and he spotted her easily. There weren't that many people at Ace in the Hole right now.

As soon as Greg sat down, a waitress came over to their table. Hadley ordered a cranberry spritzer. He ordered an expensive shot of whiskey.

"Same old Hadley," he said, teasingly.

"Same old Greg."

Hadley happened to look up at the door when the next person strode in. That person was Derek. She thought about waving to him but then considered not doing it. If he came over to the table, she'd be friendly. But she and Derek mixed like oil and water.

The waitress soon brought their drinks, and she and Greg ordered from the menu. It was obvious Greg was waiting until they didn't have interruptions to speak with her.

"You were right about no gourmet food," he said. "Tell me it's the best burger in Montana."

"It's the best burger in Montana," she said with a straight face.

He laughed. "That's another thing I like about you, Hadley. You make me laugh."

She was tired of waiting and wanted to know why he'd come. "So tell me, why this visit to Rust Creek Falls?"

"I have a proposition for you."

She studied him. There had never been anything romantic between them. Greg had preconceived ideas and could be a bit of a snob. But he'd always been kind to her and they agreed on veterinary medicine practices.

"But first I have one important question for you," he said.

"Shoot."

"Haven't you always wanted your own practice?"

"Sure, I want my own practice."

"How about having it right now? How about a partnership? How would you like to come to St. Louis and form a successful practice with me?"

"You're serious?"

"I know you, Hadley. You're interested in more than a practice in Bozeman. Think about the cultural advantages of St. Louis and a chance to see and live in another place. Big-city life would be an experience for you."

It certainly would. Hadn't she wanted to experience big-city life someday? But a practice with Greg?

She hadn't even had time to wrap her head around the idea when Derek spotted her. All smug smile and twinkling eyes, he strode toward their table, his arm in a sling.

Greg raised a questioning brow as he watched the cowboy approach.

Derek stopped at their table. "Hi, Hadley. I didn't expect to see you here."

"Hi, Derek. Just having dinner with a friend. Derek Dalton meet Greg Fordham."

Derek eyed Greg suspiciously. Maybe it was the cut of Greg's suit or the glimmer of his gold watch that caused that wary look in Derek's eyes. "I'm meeting Eli here for drinks."

Hadley could have groaned. She'd really never expected that, or this...to have to give some sort of explanation. On the other hand, she didn't owe *anybody* an explanation. This was her life, and she was going to live it as she saw fit. Eli hadn't asked her if she wanted to get together again tonight. Obviously he'd had plans with Derek.

She didn't have to involve Derek in conversation because at that moment Eli walked into the Ace in the Hole. He saw the three of them, frowned and came over to the table.

"This town is full of cowboys," Greg said, loud enough for Derek and Eli to hear.

Hadley did have the right to live her own life, but what she and Eli had shared *did* mean something. She didn't want him to think she had taken it lightly.

So she went through introductions again, ending with, "Greg and I went to veterinary school together."

Derek rolled his eyes. "I can see the three of you are probably going to be talking about horses. I think I'll just mosey over to the bar."

When Eli looked at Hadley and said politely, "Enjoy your dinner," she couldn't let him walk away. Impulsively she asked, "Won't you join us? You haven't eaten yet, have you?"

He waved at their burgers. "You've already been served."

"That doesn't matter. You know they'll bring another burger out here quick. Please join us."

Eli slung a chair around from one of the other tables and positioned it between Hadley and Greg. "Where are you from?" Eli asked, because it was obvious Greg wasn't from here.

"At present, St. Louis," Greg said formally.

Eli shed his suede jacket onto the back of his chair, revealing a plaid flannel shirt and jeans.

"So you and your brother handle steers?" Greg asked, looking as if he really wanted to know.

"We handle steers, feed horses, see to everyday workings of a ranch."

"Do you have a big spread?" Greg asked.

"It's a family spread," Eli answered truthfully, then signaled to the waitress and pointed to the burger at Hadley's place. She got the idea and nodded.

"So you all live in one big ranch house?"

Now Hadley spoke up. She didn't like Greg's tone or his questioning attitude. Eli wasn't someone to put under a microscope, even though he showed no signs of being bothered by Greg's questions. Still, she sensed the squaring of his shoulders and the straightening of his spine that said he was on guard.

"Eli and his brothers and sisters each received a parcel of land. Eli built his house on his. It's beautiful," she said. "The finest workmanship I've seen."

Greg looked from Eli to Hadley then back at Eli. "That sounds as if you worked on it yourself."

"I did. My brother's an architect, so I consulted with him."

"An architect," Greg said with a nod, as if that was something he could understand. "And where did you go to school?"

Hadley shifted in her seat as a look crossed Eli's face that was much like a shadow. She didn't understand it.

"I decided against a formal college education," Eli told Greg.

"I see," Greg said, obviously not seeing at all. "Hadley and I attended one of the best veterinary schools there is. That's why I was so surprised when she decided to practice in Bozeman."

Eli shrugged. "It seems logical she'd want to be close to home."

"After an education, home is where life takes you," Greg protested. "I've just invited her to join me in a practice in St. Louis. It would be a wonderful life experience for her. She'd be able to break out of the constraints of small-town life."

Hadley was totally surprised by that comment. "I never said I was constrained by small-town life," she said.

"You don't have to say it. It's obvious. Your mind has a much greater reach than you give yourself credit for. Once you're in a setting with culture, amenities and a more eclectic lifestyle, your horizons will broaden tremendously."

Was it true? Would her horizons broaden? Maybe. Would she be gaining rather than giving up? Or would she be losing connections she found dear and miss them so much that no experience would be worth that? Hard to know without thinking on it, without discussing it with Claire and Tessa, and maybe even her mother and grandmother.

Eli was giving her an odd look, as if Greg were unveiling a side of her that he'd never seen. Would she change if she moved to St. Louis? Did she want to change?

Greg kept talking about St. Louis as she picked at her burger. She seemed to have lost her appetite. Eli ate his with a distracted look, but every once in a while he glanced from her to Greg as if he were puzzled. She had the sudden urge to touch him, to put her hand on his forearm, to have a conversation just with him. But Greg was rattling on, and she could see Derek sitting over at the bar, watching all.

Finally, Greg wiped his mouth with his napkin and then set it on the table. "I know you need time to think about this, and also to see if you can come up with money for the investment. I wanted to present this to you before the new year. I'll email you the details." He stood. "I'd better be getting back to Kalispell. I have an early flight in the morning." He nodded to Eli. "It was nice meeting you."

Then Greg gave Hadley a cursory hug. "I'll give you a call after Christmas and we can talk about this further. If need be, maybe you could fly to St. Louis and see what I'm planning."

"I'll think about all of it," she said because

she would. She sat down again slowly as Greg left the Ace in the Hole. She felt a little bit shell-shocked by the whole evening.

She hardly had a chance to catch her breath when Eli moved his chair closer to hers.

He asked, "Did you and that guy once have something going?"

"No," she protested. "At least not in the way you mean. Greg and I had classes together. We have the same philosophy about veterinary medicine. But the closest we got was the same study group."

"You've been in touch since college?"

"Sure. Emails, catching up on what the other's doing. We're friends, Eli. Not close friends, but friends."

Eli looked as if he wanted to say something but seemed to think better of it.

"What?"

"Maybe he has a torch for you and that's why he wants you to come to St. Louis."

"You don't think this is a purely professional reason he came to see me?"

"I don't know. *You* tell *me*."

"I'm telling you. It's purely professional." Could Eli be jealous? Was that what his questions were about?

"You said you weren't serious about anyone since that Justin."

"I haven't dated since Justin," she said a bit defensively.

"For some reason Greg thinks you'd want to move to St. Louis. Is that the kind of life you want? A big city, traffic, noise?"

"A broader experience, theater, a different lifestyle?" she countered.

"A partner who thinks he knows best about everything?"

Eli had that right. But for the moment, her concentration wasn't on Greg. It was on Eli, and she didn't like where this was going. "He's given me much to think about, maybe even an opportunity. I've always wanted to have my own practice or be a partner in a practice."

"You can do that anywhere."

"Yes, I could. But why shouldn't I want more than what I have? Don't you want more than what *you* have?"

"I'm satisfied."

"Are you? Is that why you don't travel anymore? Is that why you don't rock climb? Would you even give a different kind of life a chance?"

Eli's face was stony with resolve. She

wanted to shake him or get a rise out of him. She wanted to see him as other than dependable, reliable and stoic. "Maybe I want a chance to change my life. Didn't you break off your engagement because you couldn't change yours?"

As soon as she said the words, she wished she hadn't. But the harm was done. Eli's expression told her that. He was closed down to her.

She reached for his arm. "Eli, I'm sorry."

Apparently Eli didn't want to hear any apologies from her. He didn't brush her off, but he easily broke her grasp and stood. "I'll pay for my burger at the bar. I can't criticize you because you want to experience something new. But don't tell me how I should live *my* life."

Hadley thought about going after him as he strode toward the bar, but that would be just too humiliating. She wouldn't be humiliated by a man again. However, as Eli left the Ace in the Hole and Derek followed him out, she wondered exactly what she had just done.

And if she'd ever see Eli Dalton again.

Eli wanted to ram his fist into something, but he knew that wouldn't do any good. Besides, his brother was close on his heels. They were on the street now, headed toward Eli's truck.

Eli called over his shoulder, "See you back at the ranch."

But Derek didn't stop. He kept coming. "What was that about?" his brother asked.

"None of your concern."

"It looked like it should be *somebody's* concern. Did you two have a fight?"

"Hadley received an offer to join a friend in a practice in St. Louis."

Derek whistled low. Then he muttered, "I can only imagine how much that guy's suit cost."

Eli suddenly rounded on his brother and asked, "Do you think I'm inflexible?"

Derek's mouth opened in surprise. Then he studied Eli. "Inflexible? You mean because you know what you want?"

"Yeah, something like that. Was I being inflexible because I wouldn't move to Chicago to be with Elaine?"

Derek shrugged. "I don't think that whole situation was about moving."

"No? Then what was it about?" Eli demanded to know, feeling frustrated and unsettled.

"I don't think you loved her enough to change your life."

Derek's observation hit home. As Eli thought about what he'd felt for Elaine, he said absently, "I used to enjoy rock climbing."

"Yeah. So?" Then a lightbulb seemed to go off in Derek's head. He held up a finger. "Oh. So you don't do it anymore because you did it with her?"

Eli felt shaken by that thought. "Something like that."

"And you didn't find a new hobby."

"Maybe I didn't need a hobby anymore. I had the ranch."

"And is that all you have?" Derek wanted to know.

Up until Eli had met Hadley, he'd thought the ranch was enough. Oh, sure. He'd thought about the future sometimes and having a wife and kids to share it. Maybe even buying his own place. Or maybe starting up a breeding business on the Circle D. Yet he hadn't felt in any hurry to decide.

"Do you think she's going to move to St. Louis?" Derek asked. "Her family probably won't be too fond of that idea."

"Maybe she doesn't care what her family thinks. Sometimes I get the feeling she wants to get away from them." Yet he wasn't sure exactly why.

After a few beats of silence, Eli asked, "Do you think you'll ever get married?"

Derek pointed to his chest and flashed Eli a wide grin. "Me? Why should I get married when I'm having so much fun?" But then his younger brother turned serious. "You, on the other hand... You'd make a good husband and dad."

At this moment, Eli wasn't sure whether he would or wouldn't. But he did know one thing. He now had to entertain the idea that he couldn't find a life partner because maybe he was too rigid!

Chapter 12

The following Saturday, Brooks stepped into the exam room that one of his patients had just vacated. Hadley was cleaning up.

"How did the yearly physical go with Nancy's cat?" he asked. "She can be a handful."

"Just fine. Treats are a great distraction."

He smiled. "Not only for cats. I can't tell you how much I appreciate your being here, mostly because it takes the worry from Dad that we're not overbooked."

"We're good for the next hour or so. I told Anne I'd help her decorate the office this afternoon."

"I'm sure you don't want my help with that. I'll be at the computer for a while."

Brooks had just left the exam room when Hadley's phone buzzed. Her heart skipped when she saw the number. Eli.

She'd been debating with herself all week about calling him. She'd wanted to call him. But on the other hand, with her life in such a state of flux, was there a point?

After she answered, Eli asked, "Are you speaking to me?"

"If you're speaking to me."

"I shouldn't have left like I did on Monday night."

"And I shouldn't have said what I did," she admitted.

"You were feeling defensive because I was at you about St. Louis. And maybe, just maybe, you hit the mark with me."

A man who could admit to something and apologize, too. She hadn't run into many of those.

"Are you free? Can we meet for lunch?" he asked.

She hesitated for one reason. She was falling hard for Eli. She said, "I probably shouldn't. I promised Brooks's receptionist I'd help decorate the office."

"I see," he said thoughtfully. He obviously suspected she was putting him off, and she was.

"Maybe we can coordinate our schedules another time," he suggested.

"Another time," she agreed. After goodbyes, she ended the call, feeling deeply disappointed and even sad.

A half hour later she was helping Anne Lattimore attach a garland around the reception counter when the front door to the clinic opened. To Hadley's surprise, Eli strode in.

"Need help decorating?" he asked with a smile, taking off his Stetson and hanging it on a hat peg.

Just looking at Eli made Hadley feel as if she'd received an early Christmas present. His gaze swept over her violet sweater, leggings and her practical boots. She suddenly wished she'd taken care with makeup this morning.

They were still gazing each other's way when Brooks came into the reception area. "Hi, Eli. I don't have you on my schedule."

"I came to see if Hadley would put me on *her* schedule," Eli teased. "Face-to-face seems to work better with her."

Hadley felt herself blushing. They'd been

more than face-to-face, and he was referencing that.

"She doesn't have to stay," Brooks said. "Anne and I can finish up. Our appointments are done for the day unless I get an emergency call."

In a glance, Eli took in the boxes of garland and the ornaments ready for hanging wherever a critter couldn't reach them.

"I'll help," he said. "Then you'll all get done faster."

Hadley wasn't sure what to say to that. Anne was looking back and forth between them, her eyebrows quirked. She said, "I'll go fetch the twinkle lights."

Brooks disappeared, too, and Hadley was left with Eli. He took a hammer and a tack from the counter and tapped it into the door frame. "Can you spare some time if we get this finished?"

"What did you have in mind?" she asked, her heart beating way too fast.

"How about drinks at Maverick Manor? We can talk uninterrupted."

Just what were they going to talk about? But she didn't ask that question.

He took a step closer to her. "Are you running away from me?"

"Not right now," she said with certainty. "And, yes, I'll go to Maverick Manor with you and have drinks."

He came even closer. "Ever since the other night, all I want to do is touch you."

She glanced over her shoulder. "Eli," she warned.

"I think Anne and Brooks left us alone on purpose. They seem pretty savvy about those kinds of things."

Maybe they were, but Hadley wasn't sure *she* was. She knew exactly what Eli meant. She wanted to touch him, too. After all, they'd made love. They'd been naked with each other. They'd spoken in low whispers and called each other's name at the height of passion.

Eli reached out and ran his thumb over her cheek. "I remember everything, Hadley, don't you?"

She nodded because she couldn't speak, not with Eli looking at her like that, not with him touching her this way. The brush of his thumb went deeper than skin. It went to her heart. When he bent his head and gently nibbled on her lower lip, she wrapped her arms around his neck. His kiss was prolonged and deep, and she responded to it with all of her being. She didn't know how long they kissed. She just knew all of it was romantic and heart-melting and just what she needed.

Finally, they both came up for air. He said in a husky voice, "So you have to decorate in here, huh?"

She smiled. "I do."

"Then let's get to it," he said with determination. "The faster we get done, the faster I get you to myself."

An hour later, when they left the veterinary clinic, Eli suggested they drive their own cars. It made sense to him since Hadley seemed to be in a skittish mood. She hadn't been in a skittish mood during that kiss, but other than that, he could see she felt almost awkward with him. How could that be when they'd made love so passionately?

While they'd decorated, they'd made small talk about what had happened on *The Great Roundup* last night. He'd watched the show at the Ace in the Hole again while Hadley had caught the program with Claire and Melba.

Eli wanted to erase the awkwardness. There were so many things they needed to discuss. Maybe today they would. Maybe today they'd move forward so they both knew where they stood.

Maverick Manor was a rustic hotel that had a gorgeous view of the Montana wilderness. He met Hadley in the lobby, in front of the stone fireplace that was big enough to stand in. They went into the restaurant that had been added on. It was after the lunch hour, and most of the seats and tables were empty. Eli was grateful for that, as the hostess showed them to a private table in a corner alcove. When the waitress came to take their drink orders, Eli held up the extensive wine list.

"Wine?" he asked.

But Hadley shook her head. "No, I think I'd better stay clearheaded for this conversation."

"How about an Irish coffee?" the waitress asked. "Easy on the Irish."

Hadley glanced at her. "That does sound good."

"I'll have the same," Eli said.

Once the waitress had scurried off, Eli reached across the table and took Hadley's hand. "I don't want to put you on the defensive, Hadley," he told her. "But I do have a question."

"If you're already warning me—"

"It's just that I might not have any right to ask it."

"Go ahead."

"Why didn't you tell me about the offer for the job in St. Louis? We were together the day before."

"It just came up. Remember when I got the call when we were shopping? That was Greg, and I didn't know what he was going to ask me then. He just said that he wanted to meet, that he had a proposition for me. I had no idea what that meant."

Eli studied her face and decided she was telling him the truth. He'd come to expect honesty from Hadley. "And you tried to avoid seeing me today because you thought it would be awkward?"

"Yes, it would be awkward. I never should have poked into your personal life. I shouldn't have said anything."

"You were right on the money."

Hadley looked startled for a moment.

"I don't know if rigidity was my problem, but I thought Elaine and I were building a life here. She thought she'd make a grand move and I would go with her. I was never anything but clear that my life was in Rust Creek Falls."

"Did you know she wanted more?"

"I knew she had ambition."

"If you knew she had ambition, why didn't you see the rest?"

"I don't understand."

"Just how far could ambition get her in Rust Creek Falls? She had to take it to the next level, Eli. Was she unhappy here?"

"I didn't think she was unhappy when she was with me."

"Other than you. Was she happy in her life here?"

He looked troubled. "No. She complained about a lot."

"That was the red flag that you didn't want to see. You thought you could be everything to her, and that wasn't so."

As he thought about it, he realized Hadley's conclusion was credible. He squeezed her hand. "How did you get so smart?"

"You don't want to know."

However, he *did* want to know. But he had the feeling Hadley wasn't going to tell him today. "Do you think I rigidly just don't want to move away from Rust Creek Falls and that's why I broke off the engagement?"

"Isn't that the reason?"

"No. I like my life. I like being close to my family. I like knowing what's going on with them as much as I can, and having their support and my giving mine. Tell me about your family. Don't you want to spend time with them?"

At that moment the waitress brought their Irish coffees. This gave Hadley the chance to stall, to taste the whipped cream, to stir the coffee with her spoon. But finally she looked him straight in the eye. "My family is paired off. I'm already long-distance from Tessa when she's in California. If I move away, they won't miss me."

"You're wrong, especially if you move to St. Louis. You and your sisters are close."

"We can talk on the phone and text."

"That's not the same thing as talking face-to-face, and you know it. What about your grandmother? And I'm sure your parents want you close." He let up the pressure, took a sip of the coffee and then set it back down, intending to change the subject. He didn't want to put more barriers between himself and Hadley. He wanted to break them down. "You know we're both very lucky to have large extended families. Rust Creek Falls is overrun by Daltons of late, and I couldn't be happier about that. But not everybody is so lucky."

"Are you thinking of someone in particular?"

"I'm thinking about the Stocktons. Bella and Hudson have found happiness, but Bella and her brother Jamie have been through a world of hurt because they were separated from their siblings."

"I know some of their story," Hadley said. "They were torn apart by a car accident ten years ago, right?"

"Yes. Jamie and Bella went to live with their grandparents. The older children left on their own because they were eighteen. The younger ones were adopted. Jamie and Bella had no idea where any of their brothers and sisters were. I can't imagine what it would be like to grow up not knowing where my brothers and sisters were. Just think about that hole in your heart every day, not knowing if they were okay or thriving."

"But the Stocktons recently reunited with two of their missing siblings."

Eli nodded. "Daniel and Dana. And they're still looking for the rest. They're hoping to have them all back by the time Dan marries Anne Lattimore at Christmastime."

Soft piano music had begun to play in the background, and they listened for a while as they sipped their coffee. Staring at Hadley, realizing her beauty, remembering their night together, his mind wandered off. There was a huge Christmas tree at the side of the room. It stood for everything he wanted, and maybe hadn't realized it until this moment. Staring at that tree, its glistening ornaments and its lights, he could see Hadley and himself standing there in front of it with children of their own. His mind veered on a detour to Christmas morning where they were all gathered around the tree opening presents. There was a little Eli Junior, all excited about a fancy fire truck. And a little girl who looked just like Hadley clutched a teddy bear. When Hadley entered the scene, she was rounded with child. His child. His children.

"Eli?"

Hadley had asked him a question and he must have missed it.

She asked, "Where did you just go?"

He'd taken a trip into the future, maybe the exact future he wanted. He'd looked for a woman like Hadley for a long time. Now that he'd found her, he didn't want to let her slip through his hands.

"So where did you just go?" Hadley asked him again.

He couldn't scare her off. That would defeat every purpose. And she'd been hurt before. He needed to proceed with caution. "Are you really sure you can't stay through Christmas?"

"I can't let my boss down. I told him I'd be back to cover for him by December 11."

"All right, then. If you won't be here on the twenty-fifth, then I'd like to celebrate Christmas with you ahead of time."

"I don't understand."

"I'll create Christmas just for the two of us. We'll have our own celebration before you leave."

"I don't know, Eli. There's a lot to do between now and then—"

Leaning forward, he took her hands in his and pulled them up to his face. "Say you'll let me create a celebration for the two of us...a private celebration." He kept his gaze on hers and wouldn't let her look away. She didn't.

In fact, she said, "This *could* be a Christmas celebration to remember."

"As soon as I figure out the best way to celebrate, I'll let you know. I'm thinking Friday evening would be good. Are you free?"

"I can be free."

"Then Friday evening it is. And how about we seal the deal with a kiss?"

"We're in public," she whispered.

"And no one's watching," he said, as he kissed her and she kissed him back with all the enthusiasm of their earlier kiss. He'd better come up with the best before-Christmas celebration ever and make it memorable.

Eli looked around the suite at Maverick Manor and knew everything was perfect. Hadley would be meeting him here shortly. They'd managed to meet at his cabin only twice since their drinks at Maverick Manor. Both times had left him wanting more. The problem was they'd both been a little on guard there in case they were interrupted. His family didn't always respect his boundaries.

He could have set up this Christmas celebration at his place, but he hadn't wanted to take any chances. He didn't want any interruptions. He wanted a secluded place where he and Hadley would be undisturbed. No ranch. No relatives. And if he had his way, no phones.

Understandably Hadley's memories of Christmas weren't good ones. He was going to change all that tonight. Maybe they couldn't spend Christmas Eve or Christmas Day together, but they'd have their holiday tonight—and he'd make sure it was memorable.

At the knock at the door, Eli went to answer it. When he opened it, he found Hadley, who had a puzzled expression on her face. "That was an enigmatic text," she said. "'Meet me at Maverick Manor, Room 333.' Here I am. Did you have a business meeting here or something?"

He took her hand and led her inside. "No business meeting. I decided we needed a change of venue."

Hadley's eyes widened as she gazed around the room. First she spotted the Christmas tree with its ornaments, garland and lights twinkling at her from almost every branch. A fire burned brightly in the fireplace, sending a glow throughout the room. She took a few more steps inside. Beyond the sitting area and fireplace stood a king-size lodgepole pine bed all dressed up for Christmas with a red-and-green spread. Beside it on one of the nightstands was a cooler with a bottle of wine. Flameless candles glowed here and there, adding to the holiday charm. And last, but not least, her eyes took a path back to the fireplace and its mantel. From that mantel hung a huge red stocking emblazoned with

Hadley's name. The stocking was filled to overflowing with little wrapped presents.

"Eli, what did you do?" She turned to face him, her eyes glowing bright.

"I told you I wanted to celebrate Christmas with you. This is my idea of it. I ordered room service, so dinner should be here in about fifteen minutes. How about a glass of wine to start off the evening?"

She took off her scarf and jacket, and Eli took them from her. After he laid her coat over a chair, she agreed, "A glass of wine would be lovely." She motioned to the tree and the fire. "I still can't believe you did all this."

Going to her, he wrapped his arms around her and brought her in for a kiss.

Afterward, when they were both breathing heavily, he asked, "Now do you believe it?"

She laughed. "I do. I feel like a kid on Christmas morning."

"Exactly what I was going for," he said lightly.

He'd no sooner poured the two of them a glass of wine and put the bottle back in its cooler when there was a rap on the door. It took him only a few seconds to sign for the food. He had the busboy set it up on the coffee table by the sofa.

When they were alone again and seated on the sofa, Hadley said, "I can't wait to see what you ordered."

He took the lids from both of their dinners to reveal prime rib and lobster tail, mashed potatoes, green beans almandine and crème brûlée for dessert.

"Oh my gosh, Eli. This is decadent."

"Just wait until you have butter dripping from your lips and I kiss you. Now *that's* decadent."

The look in her eyes told him that she agreed. They talked and laughed throughout their meal, but more often their eyes met and so did their lips. Buttery kisses seemed like their new best idea ever.

They fed each other crème brûlée, letting the creamy texture linger on their tongues and tasting the dessert from each other. Their kisses were becoming longer and hotter until Eli broke away, took a deep breath and said huskily, "You have to look in your stocking."

Hadley blinked at him. "Now?"

He nodded, rose from the sofa and unhooked the stocking from the mantel. He brought another package along, too, a Santa bag with a mound of white tissue. He lay the stocking on her lap. "Start with these."

As Hadley unwrapped each small package, her smiles grew broader. There were chocolate bars and gummy candies, a toy dog and cat, and a figurine of a foal with the same coloring as Coco. Hadley ran her fingers over it lovingly. "It's beautiful, Eli. Thank you. I'll never forget that moment when the foal was born, or being with you when it happened."

She'd said the words that were important for his heart to hear. Being with him had mattered. He knew being with her mattered. He handed her the bag next. "Something for tonight."

"Should I guess?" she asked with a sexy look in her eyes.

If she was expecting red or black lace, she was going to be surprised, he thought.

And surprised she was. Her eyes widened, her cheeks grew rosy with delight, and her smile blessed his soul. She carefully unfolded a cozy fleece nightshirt embroidered with a puppy wearing a Santa hat. Hadley laughed, and Eli knew he had hit just the right note.

"Stay here tonight with me?" Eli asked, knowing her answer could tell him everything he needed to know.

"This could be our last night together," she murmured.

"Don't think about that," he suggested, still waiting for her answer.

"Yes, I'll stay." Then teasingly she asked, "Are we going to watch *The Great Roundup*?"

"Not tonight," Eli murmured as he took her into his arms and kissed her.

That kiss fueled their passion. She couldn't seem to rid him of his clothes fast enough nor he hers. They dropped their clothes on the way to the bed and hardly made it there. Eli's groans seemed to quicken her hands as she stroked his muscles, his skin, every part of him. When his tongue drove into her mouth, she took him, tasted him, nibbled at his lips, too.

They seemed to burn for each other. The curve of Hadley's neck was perfect for his kisses. Her shoulders were creamy pink, so feminine yet so strong, too. She was the type of woman who could face adversity and win. As Hadley sifted her hand through his chest hair, she made him crazy with need. Wherever Hadley touched him, it wasn't only pleasure but torment. He wanted satisfaction as much as she did, but he wasn't willing to rush to get there. She might be arousing him, but each brush of his hand on her skin aroused her, too. Her breaths were shallow, her pulse was racing and his name was on her lips.

He'd never felt before what he was feeling with Hadley, and that's what drove him on. He coaxed sighs from her. He kissed her until all of her skin had a rosy glow.

Finally, Hadley seemed to be at her limit. Her hands gripped his shoulders, and she said, "Let go, Eli. I want you. Can't you see that?"

"I see that," he said with some satisfaction. "And I want you, too."

She arched toward him, but still he wouldn't hurry. He entered her with a slowness that drove them both crazy. And then, finally, they found the pleasure they were seeking. The release, when it came, seemed to shatter them both.

Hadley held on to Eli as if she'd never let him go. And that's what he wanted. He didn't want her to ever let go. That was almost his last conscious thought. Almost. Because there was one other, and he knew exactly what he was going to do.

Chapter 13

Hadley had never had a more perfect night. She'd never been loved the way Eli had loved her—with care, with passion, with gentleness. She'd worn her nightgown with the puppy in the Santa hat as they shared a midnight snack. And then he'd removed it and they'd started all over again. Now they were dressed and having the full breakfast he'd ordered for them from room service. Sitting next to him on the couch, she couldn't stop smiling as they drank orange juice, ate scrambled eggs and croissants, and sipped coffee. She hated to leave, but she knew she had to. She'd told Brooks she'd be in this morning.

All of a sudden, Eli said, "I want to ask you something very important."

She thought he might ask when she'd be back after Christmas. She thought he might ask if they could see each other again before she left tomorrow. She thought...

Suddenly Eli pushed their breakfast tray back on the coffee table. Then he stood. He was towering over her, looking a little uncertain. And she had no clue as to what he was thinking. She had no clue until he pushed the coffee table away and got down on one knee in front of her.

Taking her hand in his, he said, "I'd like to wake up every morning the way we woke up this morning. I hadn't planned on doing this just yet. I know you might have doubts, but I don't, and I need you to know that. I want you to stay in Rust Creek Falls and start a future with me. I'd like you to marry me. Will you, Hadley?"

Hadley had never had a panic attack in her life. But right now, her breaths were short and shallow, her chest felt tight and she didn't know if she could suck in another lungful of air. She was looking at Eli and the hope in his face. She felt joy that he wanted to marry her. Yet she also felt panic and so much fear.

Could this possibly be the real thing? Just asking that, her thoughts went back to that Vegas chapel and how hard she'd fallen the last time, and how badly it had all turned out. Justin had impulsively proposed, too!

Eli was still on one knee, gazing at her, waiting for an answer.

She wanted to say yes. Oh, how much she wanted to say yes. But she knew she couldn't. She had to let him down easy. She had to make this easier for both of them.

Finding her voice, she murmured, "We hardly know each other."

He squeezed her hand. "I know this is fast. Yet I feel like I *do* know you. And I think I know you very well. I know you like cream in your coffee with a dab of sugar. I know secretly you like cats more than you like dogs. I know that although you complain about them, your family is important to you, and that Claire is probably your best friend. I know that you like to cook, and you like to be kissed on the nape of your neck. I know you can drive a stick shift, and you prefer boots with a fleece lining."

He was still smiling, and she knew she had to wipe that smile away. She knew she had to disappoint him, and that by disappointing him, she might be turning away a future with him. But what choice did she have? No one knew her secret. Absolutely no one. But she had to tell Eli and hurt them both.

She cleared her throat and tried to take all emotion out of her voice. "You do know those things about me. But you don't know *everything*."

"What else could I possibly need to know?" he teased.

"You need to know that I've been married before."

Eli's smile faded into a frown. His brows drew together, and she knew he was trying to decide what to say. Finally, he asked, "Why didn't you say anything before now?"

Feeling defensive, feeling as if the bottom were falling out of her world, feeling as if everything she'd hidden for so long was going to be made public, she said tersely, "We haven't known each other all that long. I didn't feel it was necessary."

At that Eli got to his feet and sat on the sofa beside her. He went silent.

She knew what he was thinking. He disapproved. Maybe he thought she'd never been seriously in love. Possibly he thought she was still in love with her ex. She could certainly disabuse him of that notion, but what good would that do? He disapproved, that was obvious, and he didn't even know the worst of it yet. But why tell him the whole sorry tale? Why humiliate herself further? How could she ever admit to Eli how badly she'd been duped by Justin? He'd know then she was a poor judge of character. He'd know then that her impulses had gotten her into a peck of trouble. He'd realize even further that she wasn't the woman he thought she was.

Sparing herself the indignity of admitting all of it, she rose to her feet. Her coat was still lying over the chair where he'd put it last night. She went to it, picked it up, then pulled her purse from the end table.

She knew her voice was stilted when she said, "Eli, thank you for my Christmas celebration. I do appreciate it. I really do." Then she swung around, headed for the door and left. She practically ran down the hall, and she knew she was going to keep running until she reached Bozeman.

When the door closed behind Hadley, Eli felt as if he were in shock. She'd been married?

Restless, unsure what to do next, he paced

around the suite studying the remnants of the night they'd shared—the tousled sheets, the condom wrappers on the nightstand, the empty wineglasses.

Then he spotted what made him saddest of all. Hadley had left the nightshirt that he'd bought for her, the one embroidered with the dog in the Santa hat.

She'd been so cool when she'd left. Had he imagined last night?

His mind raced. Part of his mind had told him she was too good to be true. This was like the other shoe dropping. This was like Elaine saying she was moving to Chicago. This was like—

This was like he'd fallen and Hadley hadn't. Maybe she was still in love with her ex-husband. Maybe he was a fool for thinking he'd really known her. Worse yet, maybe he was just plain stupid for making her into something she wasn't. Did she even care for him? That blank expression when she'd left—

He'd never seen her look like that before. An ex-husband? How long had she been married? Was this the guy who had dumped her? Had he served her with divorce papers on Christmas Eve?

Eli had questions, and he needed answers. But first he had to figure out what was real and what wasn't.

Hadley had put in the morning with Brooks, going through the motions, letting her training and experience guide her, doing all the right things at the right times. But she'd really just been biding her time until she could leave. When she made a promise, she kept it, professionally and otherwise. So she hadn't wanted to let Brooks down. But when he'd said she could leave at noon, she'd taken the opportunity to do just that.

At the boardinghouse, she was so glad that everything seemed quiet. Everybody was busy doing Christmas errands, all except for her grandmother, who was working on reservations for the new year.

She told her grandmother she had to get going today instead of tomorrow and she'd be down to say goodbye as soon as she'd packed. It didn't take long. As she said goodbye, her grandmother tried to delay her with a question. "Is everything all right?"

Hadley assured her it was and made her way out, till she ran into Old Gene. He took one look at her and asked, "What's the matter?"

"I'm fine. I just want to get back to Bozeman and take care of things since I've been away."

Gene scrutinized her more carefully. "You were gone last night. How's Eli?"

She couldn't prevaricate with her grandfather. "Eli is fine."

"Too much *fine* going around," Old Gene said. "Why are you rushing off today instead of tomorrow if both of you are fine? Shouldn't he see you off or something?"

All right. So she had to tell him. "Eli and I probably won't be seeing each other anymore. Now I really have to get going, okay?"

"Your sister is going to be calling you," he warned her.

And she knew what that meant. He was going to tell Claire exactly what she'd said and Claire would probably tell Tessa. But for now, she just had to escape. So she gave her grandfather a kiss on the cheek, climbed into her SUV and headed for Bozeman.

The drive didn't do much to calm her. Too many times she found tears rolling down her cheeks and she swiped them away. At her apartment, she gathered up all the mail that had accumulated on the floor when the postman had slipped it through the mail slot in the door. She sorted through it to give herself something to do. Nothing of importance there. She unpacked in sort of a daze, still thinking about Eli down on one knee…still thinking about last night…still thinking about the way he'd held her and kissed her and touched her.

So she was startled when her cell phone buzzed. She saw the caller was Tessa and thought about letting the call go to voice mail. But she'd have to deal with her sisters eventually.

After she answered, Tessa asked, "What happened with Eli?"

"We…broke up," Hadley said lamely. Then she murmured, "It was never that serious."

"I don't believe you."

"Not my problem," Hadley shot back.

"Yes, it is if you aren't being honest with yourself," Tessa said. "Every relationship has bumps. Work things out with him."

"There's nothing to work out," she insisted.

"What did he do?"

"He didn't *do* anything."

"Then why did you break up? You know, Carson and I faced troubles, and we got through them. Claire and Levi have certainly had theirs. But their marriage is stronger than ever. You and Eli are a perfect couple."

"Tessa—" Hadley's voice broke.

"Tell me," Tessa prompted.

Eli knew now. Maybe it was time everybody knew. "Three years ago I got married."

"You *what*?"

"I met Justin at a veterinary convention in Las Vegas. He was a pharmaceutical rep. We had a few meetings together, sat in on workshops, had lunch together every day. More than lunch. We were so attracted to each other. I came back to Bozeman, but we were on the phone together every day. We were just so hot for each other, so I flew back out to Las Vegas. We got married in one of the wedding chapels. I should have known something was wrong when Justin convinced me we shouldn't tell our families until we could meet them in person."

"So you were secretly married," Tessa repeated slowly.

"Yes, and it was thrilling. The sex was phenomenal. But when I said we should fly back together to tell all of you the happy news, Justin just kept postponing that. Finally, one night after he'd made another excuse, I went online and searched him."

"You Googled your husband?"

"I should have done it before he became my husband because then I would have found out he was already married to someone else."

"Oh, Hadley. What did you do? Did you press charges?"

"Press charges? All I wanted to do was curl up in a ball and die. I couldn't understand how I'd been so *stupid*. But I had a life to live and a job to keep, so I hired a discreet attorney and was divorced. But I haven't trusted a man since. You know, I keep suspecting they're not what they seem. At least I didn't trust anyone until Eli."

"Are you sure you don't want me to beat up this jerk or have him arrested?"

Hadley knew Tessa was probably only *half* kidding. "No, it's over and done."

"Sis, you can't let your past determine your future. What did you tell Eli?"

"All I told him was that I'd been married before. That seemed to be enough of a shock for him. I couldn't tell him the rest. And I don't even know if he really loved me or just said he did."

"He told you he loved you?"

"Well, not in so many words, but he asked me to marry him."

"Hadley. You've got to tell him *all* of it."

"No, I don't. It's embarrassing and it's humiliating. It's bad enough it was a shock that I told him I was married before. To tell him I was married to a bigamist?"

"Mom and Dad don't know about this?"

"No one knows about this. No one. And I want to keep it that way. Promise me you won't say anything to Eli or the rest of the family."

"It's going to come out, Hadley."

"Maybe, maybe not. Please, just don't tell anyone."

"I can't promise."

"You have to promise."

"Let me tell Claire."

"If you tell Claire, she'll tell Levi. If you tell Claire, she'll let it slip to Grandmother."

Tessa was silent for a few moments. Then she said, "I'm going to give you a few days to think about this. But I hope you'll change your mind. I hope you'll let me bring it all out into the open because that's really what you need to do."

"I'll think about your advice," Hadley said, knowing she would. And that's the way they left it because they were sisters…because they trusted each other…because they would always have each other's backs.

Eli checked the app on his phone the following Friday evening. The map said he was here. According to Tessa, Hadley rented the first floor of a two-story Federal-style house in Bozeman. He'd been miserable since she'd left…since he hadn't stopped her from leaving. And why hadn't he?

Because he had a past, too, and apparently, just like Hadley, it was affecting his future. Tessa's call had made him bump up right against that. They hadn't had a long conversation, but essentially she told Eli if he wanted a future with Hadley, he had to fight for it.

He'd done a lot of thinking over the past week. He hadn't been wrong about his feelings for Hadley. And he suspected she had feelings for him but was afraid of them. Tessa had said as much. She hadn't told him any more of Hadley's story. She said that was for her sister to do. But if he'd judged Hadley from the moment she'd started to tell him that she had been married before, that's why Hadley had run.

Had he been judging her or himself? He hadn't meant to judge her. He'd just been so shocked. But before making this drive he promised himself he would not be shocked again, no matter what Hadley told him. Because whatever her romantic history was, it simply didn't matter. He loved her, and he had to make her see that. He had to make her see that they both had to fight for what they wanted.

As he strode up the walk to the door, he realized she could still be at the veterinary clinic where she worked. After all, she said she was covering for her boss.

He rang the bell, not knowing what to expect. When Hadley opened the door, her eyes went wide and her mouth rounded in an O. She was wearing a red sweater and green leggings with black boots and looked delicious.

"I didn't know if you'd be home," he started.

"I just got home," she said.

"May I come in?"

She looked embarrassed for a moment, but she backed up and motioned to her living room. It was comfortably furnished in blues and tans and yellows. But as he looked around, he got the distinct feeling Hadley didn't spend much time here.

"Tessa called me," he said.

Hadley turned and walked away from him. "So you came because Tessa called? I'll strangle her."

"No need to do that. She just decided to give me what-for, that's all."

"I don't understand," Hadley said. "She doesn't know you."

"No, but she wants to get to know me because she asked me a very important question."

"Which was?" Hadley inquired.

"If I love you enough to fight for you."

At that, Hadley's whole body stilled and her gaze set on his. She studied his face as if she'd never see it again.

"You look as if you haven't gotten much sleep," she noticed.

"I can say the same about you. Maybe we've both been suffering needlessly. I tried to let you go because I thought I made another mistake. I thought you didn't care like I did. Your sister didn't say much. She just said we needed to talk face-to-face, and I realized how true that was."

"Let's sit," Hadley said, going to the sofa. "Or do you want something to drink first?"

He followed her and sat. "Nothing to drink. I want you to tell me whatever you need to tell me."

She must have been nervous about doing that because she inhaled a very deep breath. "All right," she agreed, blowing it out. "For three years I've kept this secret. My family doesn't know. I just told Tessa everything, and she probably told Claire. Next I'll have to tell my parents and my grandparents."

"Hadley, nothing can be that bad. They love you."

"Yes, they love me, but I didn't want them to think less of me. I'm humiliated and embarrassed by what happened."

Eli unbuttoned his jacket and shrugged out of it. He wanted to give her the plain message that he wasn't going anywhere, no matter what she had to tell him. "I'm listening," he said, reaching for her hand and holding it.

But she pulled away, obviously unsure of what his reaction would be. Somehow he had to reassure her that he loved her. That would come.

"It's not really complicated," Hadley said. "I married a bigamist. He was already married when he married me."

That wasn't something Eli had expected. "Is he in jail?" he asked angrily. "How could he do that to you?"

"I don't know," she admitted.

Eli fought the urge to reach for her hand. Instead, his eyes pleading with hers, he said, "Tell me what happened."

And she did. She ended with, "So we kept up a long-distance marriage until…until I finally got suspicious…until I did some research…until I found out he was married."

Eli couldn't help reaching for Hadley now.

He took her hand and wouldn't let her pull away. "What did you do?"

"I just wanted out. I found an attorney who handled it all discreetly. Actually, I think he threatened Justin with public humiliation and jail time. I didn't care. I just wanted to be free of him. And I was. And nobody knew about it. I'm sorry I didn't tell you earlier. I'm sorry I didn't trust you enough to tell you. But I didn't know where we were headed… or how you felt."

"That's my fault. I can't even imagine how much pain the whole thing caused you. Because of it, I can certainly understand why you turned down my impulsive wedding proposal. I can wait as long as you need me to wait to be convinced we have staying power. I'll move to Bozeman or St. Louis if that's what you want."

She looked totally shocked, totally amazed, totally radiant. "Oh, Eli, you don't have to move to Bozeman or St. Louis. I already turned down the partnership with Greg. That just wasn't right for me. But I did something yesterday."

"What?" Eli asked, because she sounded hopeful.

"I spoke to Brooks about coming on staff

in Rust Creek Falls permanently. Or there is another option. I could buy his dad's practice. I don't know if I can pull together enough money."

"Yes, you can, because I'll help you if that's what you want. Are you sure Rust Creek Falls is where you want to be?"

"It would be great to be near Tessa and Claire and my grandparents. And I'm not that far from my parents in Bozeman. And, of course, I need to be near you. I love you, Eli. I really do."

Eli drew her into his arms then. As he kissed her, he realized all of his dreams could come true.

When he carried her to her bedroom and made slow, sweet love to her, he knew they could live anywhere and it would be home. Would Hadley feel that way, too?

After a storm of passion they both fervently gave in to, they lay face-to-face in the bed. Eli pushed Hadley's hair away from her face. "If you bought Brooks's dad's practice, would you want to live in his house?"

"I don't know. I want to be with you."

He nodded. "And I want to be with you. I was just thinking, my place is more of a bachelor pad. I'm pretty sure Derek would like to move into it. Barrett Smith's place is more of a family house. We could raise a family there."

"I can see little Elis running around the property," she said with a laugh.

"And I can see little Hadleys learning how to ride a horse, wanting maybe too much freedom too early."

"You'd really give up the house you built?"

"It's a house, Hadley. I want a *home* with you. So I'm going to ask you again, and you can take all the time in the world to answer. Will you marry me?"

"I don't need time, Eli. Yes, I'll marry you!"

He kissed her again, knowing this Christmas would be one to remember for a lifetime.

* * * * *

Get 4 FREE REWARDS!

We'll send you 2 FREE Books plus 2 FREE Mystery Gifts.

Both the **Harlequin® Historical** and **Harlequin® Romance** series feature compelling novels filled with emotion and simmering romance.

YES! Please send me 2 FREE novels from the Harlequin Historical or Harlequin Romance series and my 2 FREE gifts (gifts are worth about $10 retail). After receiving them, if I don't wish to receive any more books, I can return the shipping statement marked "cancel." If I don't cancel, I will receive 6 brand-new Harlequin Historical books every month and be billed just $5.94 each in the U.S. or $6.49 each in Canada, a savings of at least 12% off the cover price or 4 brand-new Harlequin Romance Larger-Print every month and be billed just $5.84 each in the U.S. or $5.99 each in Canada, a savings of at least 14% off the cover price. It's quite a bargain! Shipping and handling is just 50¢ per book in the U.S. and $1.25 per book in Canada.* I understand that accepting the 2 free books and gifts places me under no obligation to buy anything. I can always return a shipment and cancel at any time by calling the number below. The free books and gifts are mine to keep no matter what I decide.

Choose one: ☐ **Harlequin Historical**   ☐ **Harlequin Romance Larger-Print**
                 (246/349 HDN GRAE)   (119/319 HDN GRAQ)

Name (please print)

Address   Apt. #

City   State/Province   Zip/Postal Code

Email· Please check this box ☐ if you would like to receive newsletters and promotional emails from Harlequin Enterprises ULC and its affiliates. You can unsubscribe anytime.

Mail to the **Harlequin Reader Service:**
IN U.S.A.: P.O. Box 1341, Buffalo, NY 14240-8531
IN CANADA: P.O. Box 603, Fort Erie, Ontario L2A 5X3

Want to try 2 free books from another series! Call 1-800-873-8635 or visit www.ReaderService.com.

Get 4 FREE REWARDS!

We'll send you 2 FREE Books <u>plus</u> 2 FREE Mystery Gifts.

FREE Value Over **$20**

Both the **Romance** and **Suspense** collections feature compelling novels written by many of today's bestselling authors.

YES! Please send me 2 FREE novels from the Essential Romance or Essential Suspense Collection and my 2 FREE gifts (gifts are worth about $10 retail). After receiving them, if I don't wish to receive any more books, I can return the shipping statement marked "cancel." If I don't cancel, I will receive 4 brand-new novels every month and be billed just $7.24 each in the U.S. or $7.49 each in Canada. That's a savings of up to 38% off the cover price. It's quite a bargain! Shipping and handling is just 50¢ per book in the U.S. and $1.25 per book in Canada.* I understand that accepting the 2 free books and gifts places me under no obligation to buy anything. I can always return a shipment and cancel at any time by calling the number below. The free books and gifts are mine to keep no matter what I decide.

Choose one: ☐ **Essential Romance** (194/394 MDN GQ6M) ☐ **Essential Suspense** (191/391 MDN GQ6M)

Name (please print)

Address   Apt. #

City   State/Province   Zip/Postal Code

Email: Please check this box ☐ if you would like to receive newsletters and promotional emails from Harlequin Enterprises ULC and its affiliates. You can unsubscribe anytime.

Mail to the **Harlequin Reader Service:**
IN U.S.A.: P.O. Box 1341, Buffalo, NY 14240-8531
IN CANADA: P.O. Box 603, Fort Erie, Ontario L2A 5X3

Want to try 2 free books from another series? Call 1-800-873-8635 or visit www.ReaderService.com.

---

*Terms and prices subject to change without notice. Prices do not include sales taxes, which will be charged (if applicable) based on your state or country of residence. Canadian residents will be charged applicable taxes. Offer not valid in Quebec. This offer is limited to one order per household. Books received may not be as shown. Not valid for current subscribers to the Essential Romance or Essential Suspense Collection. All orders subject to approval. Credit or debit balances in a customer's account(s) may be offset by any other outstanding balance owed by or to the customer. Please allow 4 to 6 weeks for delivery. Offer available while quantities last.

Your Privacy—Your information is being collected by Harlequin Enterprises ULC, operating as Harlequin Reader Service. For a complete summary of the information we collect, how we use this information and to whom it is disclosed, please visit our privacy notice located at corporate.harlequin.com/privacy-notice. From time to time we may also exchange your personal information with reputable third parties. If you wish to opt out of this sharing of your personal information, please visit readerservice.com/consumerschoice or call 1-800-873-8635. **Notice to California Residents**—Under California law, you have specific rights to control and access your data. For more information on these rights and how to exercise them, visit corporate.harlequin.com/california-privacy.

STRS22R2

Get 4 FREE REWARDS!

We'll send you 2 FREE Books plus 2 FREE Mystery Gifts.

FREE Value Over **$20**

Both the **Harlequin Intrigue®** and **Harlequin® Romantic Suspense** series feature compelling novels filled with heart-racing action-packed romance that will keep you on the edge of your seat.

YES! Please send me 2 **FREE** novels from the Harlequin Intrigue or Harlequin Romantic Suspense series and my 2 **FREE** gifts (gifts are worth about $10 retail). After receiving them, if I don't wish to receive any more books, I can return the shipping statement marked "cancel." If I don't cancel, I will receive 6 brand-new Harlequin Intrigue Larger-Print books every month and be billed just $6.24 each in the U.S. or $6.74 each in Canada, a savings of at least 14% off the cover price or 4 brand-new Harlequin Romantic Suspense books every month and be billed just $5.24 each in the U.S. or $5.99 each in Canada, a savings of at least 13% off the cover price. It's quite a bargain! Shipping and handling is just 50¢ per book in the U.S. and $1.25 per book in Canada.* I understand that accepting the 2 free books and gifts places me under no obligation to buy anything. I can always return a shipment and cancel at any time by calling the number below. The free books and gifts are mine to keep no matter what I decide.

Choose one: ☐ **Harlequin Intrigue Larger-Print** (199/399 HDN GRA2)   ☐ **Harlequin Romantic Suspense** (240/340 HDN GRCE)

Name (please print)

Address   Apt. #

City   State/Province   Zip/Postal Code

Email: Please check this box ☐ if you would like to receive newsletters and promotional emails from Harlequin Enterprises ULC and its affiliates. You can unsubscribe anytime.

> ### Mail to the **Harlequin Reader Service:**
> **IN U.S.A.:** P.O. Box 1341, Buffalo, NY 14240-8531
> **IN CANADA:** P.O. Box 603, Fort Erie, Ontario L2A 5X3

Want to try 2 free books from another series! Call 1-800-873-8635 or visit www.ReaderService.com.

*Terms and prices subject to change without notice. Prices do not include sales taxes, which will be charged (if applicable) based on your state or country of residence. Canadian residents will be charged applicable taxes. Offer not valid in Quebec. This offer is limited to one order per household. Books received may not be as shown. Not valid for current subscribers to the Harlequin Intrigue or Harlequin Romantic Suspense series. All orders subject to approval. Credit or debit balances in a customer's account(s) may be offset by any other outstanding balance owed by or to the customer. Please allow 4 to 6 weeks for delivery. Offer available while quantities last.

Your Privacy—Your information is being collected by Harlequin Enterprises ULC, operating as Harlequin Reader Service. For a complete summary of the information we collect, how we use this information and to whom it is disclosed, please visit our privacy notice located at corporate.harlequin.com/privacy-notice. From time to time we may also exchange your personal information with reputable third parties. If you wish to opt out of this sharing of your personal information, please visit readerservice.com/consumerschoice or call 1-800-873-8635. **Notice to California Residents**—Under California law, you have specific rights to control and access your data. For more information on these rights and how to exercise them, visit corporate.harlequin.com/california-privacy.

HIHRS22R2

HARLEQUIN
PLUS

Announcing a **BRAND-NEW**
multimedia subscription service
for romance fans like you!

Read, Watch and Play.

Experience the easiest way to get
the romance content you crave.

Start your **FREE 7 DAY TRIAL** at
www.harlequinplus.com/freetrial.